DICKHEADS & DEBAUCHERY

AND OTHER INGENIOUS WAYS TO DIE

BY

VIC FERRARI

Book layout by www.ebooklaunch.com

For my parents, who sacrificed so much for me.
I miss you both and think of you every day.

Table of Contents

Chapter 1

We All Have to Die But What's Your Rush?

Dickheads & Debauchery sounds like the name of a dive bar in a rough part of town. Although, in today's society, no city would have the balls to issue a business license with that name, so you're going to have to settle for the book. Speaking of which, you just spent $3.99 and are probably wondering if you made a wise decision.

Granted, spending $3.99 isn't going to kill you, but who likes to throw money out the window? The good news is that this book is going to provide you with a lot of laughs just by pointing out idiotic behavior most of us have engaged in, behavior that could shorten or end our lives.

For the most part, we all take our lives for granted. Some more than others, but during one time or another, everyone has engaged in some form of debauchery or has been a dickhead. Speeding, drinking, or streaking, we all have taken a shortcut or done something so blatantly stupid that we are lucky to be alive.

Most of us do not like to think about death because that's someone else's problem. Nobody wants to face life's last dance. No one in their right mind wants to die because if you do, you could miss out on something. Unless you're a manic depressive, you really shouldn't give dying much thought until you have a close call with death or when it calls for someone you know. One would think that with how much man has evolved, and the invention of the internet, someone somewhere would have come up with a cure for dying.

I myself never really thought about my own mortality until I hit my mid-forties. Death happened to other people, not to me. I was exempt from death, in my mind, I was never going to get old. I worked in law enforcement for over twenty years as a NYPD cop and detective and was exposed to plenty of death, but I naively never thought it applied to me.

I guess if I had given death a lot of thought when I was a cop, it would have made me second guess my split second decision making. And if you choose poorly in a split second, life or death scenario in law enforcement, you're going down for a dirt nap never to get up.

Death is a terrible and inevitable reality that's going to happen to all of us. None of us are getting out of this world alive; we all reach the end of the line, morta, no mas, etc. It is going to happen at some point and all we can do is try to delay it. My mother used to say, "death is so final". It's a simplistic and very accurate statement. It's going to get us all somehow, someday, eventually, but there are those dickheads who foolishly race to the front of the line to greet it. Once you're dead, you're dead. No shaman or condemned man on the green mile blowing flies out of his mouth can bring you back.

The good news however is that it's possible to put off your death and prolong your life. Believe it or not, common sense has a lot to do with how long you're going to live, survival of the fittest, that sort of thing. Common sense is not always common and often gets overlooked.

This book is definitely not going to make you any smarter, especially if you get the humor because you're already there. If you don't get the humor, that's too bad, and it probably means that people have been laughing at you your whole life.

I wanted to write a book that would make you laugh and think at the same time. The kind of book you can pick up at any page and have a laugh to get you through the day. The book is not going to give you a purpose or improve your life through positive thinking, I'm a retired cop, not Joel Osteen. This is more of a read-on-the-throne kind of book. Reader's Digest used to say "laughter is the best medicine", and I hope you have an overdose!

If you are offended easily, you may not like the book. If you believe in junk science and are under the impression that pharmaceutical companies are keeping the cure for cancer from the general public, you're not going to like the book. If you believe fat, drunken, red faced men wearing top hats and overcoats in Pennsylvania, pulling vermin from a fake den on February 2nd is an accurate way to gauge the length of winter, you're an idiot and won't understand the humor. Lastly, if you're driving a Smart Car with a coexist bumper sticker on it, you're definitely not going to like the book.

The point I am trying to make is if you do not have a sense of humor, the book is not for you. We all make mistakes and this one cost you $3.99.

Seeing Is Believing

From the beginning of time, man has been trying to figure out what happens after we die. Different religions believe different things and who can say if any of them are wrong. It all depends on your faith. Comedian George Carlin brilliantly said, "Tell people there's an invisible man in the sky who created the universe, and the vast majority will believe you. Tell them the paint is wet, and they have to touch it".

We all would like to believe there is something after this world because if we accept the concept that this is it, it makes our demise that much scarier.

I am a confused Catholic who really can't wrap my head around why a good person who leads an exemplary life would die before some scumbag criminal who brought pain and suffering to the world. God fearing people will tell you "it was their time" or "God needed them".

How many people does God really need up in heaven? If God is the Almighty and created everything in the universe, why would he take a 25 year old plumber and father of 3 up to heaven prematurely? Do the toilets clog in heaven? Does St. Peter break God's balls about wanting sensor faucets installed? I can see God leaving us with an abundance of schmucks here on earth, but I'm pretty sure there are more than enough general contractors in heaven that can handle any job.

I'm also pretty sure there is more talent in heaven than there is here on earth. So how many people does God really need up there? I am not saying I don't believe in God, but the logic about him or her seems flawed. I do believe in God to a point and I guess and I'm hedging my bets, which may or may not help me if there is an afterlife.

I have had mixed results praying to God. Sometimes God has answered my prayers when I've reached out to him, other times my calls went straight to voicemail.

We'd all like to think we are going to die on our own terms. Most of us would like to believe we will be very old, passing quietly in our sleep surrounded by loved ones who had a chance to say their final goodbyes.

Some will die quite unexpectedly through no fault of their own. Be it by accidents, acts of God, or just bad luck. Others will die prematurely and be the last to know while everyone around them could see their demise coming from a mile away.

The reality is people rarely die on their own terms. People like to believe they always have more time because death is going to get someone else before it comes for them.

Most of us usually start giving death some serious thought when we get older and our loved ones begin to pass on. We believe time is infinite and we put off life's most important things until it's too late.

Telling your parents you love them or saying sorry to someone you care about; that you've been putting off. Taking half a day to have your last will and testament written to save your grieving family from that one greedy sibling of low moral character who feels he or she is not getting their fair share; you're too busy for that.

It's almost as if your death has been predetermined like a fixed lottery and you're the last one to know that you're holding a worthless ticket that is your life. The sad thing is that for most people, seeing is believing. If like in the movies you could see in Technicolor how and when you would die, you would most certainly live your life differently.

Would you leave your house for work one morning knowing you were minutes away from being killed in a painful car accident? That would be a nice heads up, wouldn't it be? I would take the whole week off just to make sure the asshole who was scheduled to kill me with his car hit someone else.

If you knew drinking alcohol would leave you with Alzheimer's and in some crappy assisted living facility wearing a diaper, getting smacked in the head with a rolled up newspaper by your

Haitian LPN who you affectionately call "mom", would you ever drink again? You probably wouldn't touch an O'Doul's.

If on the day you were born you received your death certificate already filled out with your tentative expiration date and cause of death, would you live your life more carefully? You bet your ass you would. You would do everything in your power to lengthen your life in an effort to prove the death certificate wrong.

You would eat better, exercise and not take as many chances. You wouldn't stay out past 11pm, drink and drive, and you would wear your seatbelt. You wouldn't get on a ladder alone or decide to take up hang gliding.

You wouldn't eat that fourth pork chop at your neighbor's barbecue while flirting with the married woman whose husband with facial tattoos looks like he's one beer away from being on America's Most Wanted.

After age forty, you would get a colonoscopy every five years and figure out how to get leafy green vegetables into your body whether you like them or not.

Man has been doing ridiculous things to shorten his life long before he could walk upright. One would think we would have evolved into something a lot more superior after all this time but here you are reading this book. Ignoring the rules of common sense and swimming against actuarial tables, man has tempted fate time and time again, usually coming up short.

So why should you listen to me? Well as of this printing, I am still alive and have made it to fifty by the skin of my teeth. As a reformed dickhead, I hope to have many more birthdays.

If you want to have some laughs and avoid dying, this is the book for you.

Chapter 2

The Cancer

The Bronx is the only place in the United States that has "The" in front of it. I dare you to try, but you're going to get a headache and still not be able to think of anything. The Brooklyn, The Queens, The California… it just doesn't sound right. Growing up in "The Bronx" in the 1970s, I was taught a language Rosetta Stone has yet to translate.

Residents of The Bronx also place "The" in front of a vast variety of diseases, ailments, and treatments. "The crabs", "The AIDS", and "The plague" all were named and probably originated in The Bronx. None however is more feared than "The Cancer". Just the mention of the dreaded disease strikes fear in every man, woman, and child. It's gotten to the point that when I hear some poor bastard has been diagnosed with The Cancer, I am overcome with a perverse sense of relief it wasn't me who was diagnosed with it.

The Cancer is a real life boogeyman who can strike anyone, anytime, without warning in a variety of ways. Way back when before modern medicine developed diagnostic tests to detect cancer, it just kind of snuck up on you and before you knew it, it was too late to do anything about it. I remember as a kid, when I heard the adults speaking about The Cancer, it usually meant somebody was on the way out and their relatives were calling the funeral parlor.

A family friend was a world renowned cancer research scientist who devoted over forty years of his life to try to find a cure for this terrible disease. Oddly enough, at my grandfather's funeral, I decided to pick his brain about The Cancer, asking what it was and why it was so difficult to treat. I was about fifteen years old at the time and listened in awe as this brilliant man and a giant in cancer research took the time to explain to me one of life's terrible mysteries.

He explained The Cancer to me in layman's terms, or as much as a fifteen year old at a funeral could comprehend.

"Your body is made up of living cells that are constantly created and dying. The problem begins when there is a hiccup in your system and your body begins producing rogue cells. These cells continue to grow at a rapid rate, refusing to die, and wreaking havoc on your body."

His explanation was simple enough to me. The Cancer sounded like a badass hitman croaking people and should be avoided at all costs. After so many years he dedicated to searching for a cure for cancer, he sadly lost his life to it.

Among all the ways to die discussed in this book, The Cancer is the toughest adversary. If you google The Cancer you'll find pages of information covering possible causes and treatments. Since there is no known cure for the disease, there are plenty of people out there, credible and not, making all sorts of claims. The problem with all this information is who are you going to believe?

On one end of the spectrum, you have respected doctors with unimpeachable credentials who spent years putting together and publishing double blind studies to link the disease to possible causes. On the other side, you have the self-serving charlatan quack who claims that consuming shark cartilage or rubbing charcoal on your body will cure you of the disease.

Ask poor Andy Kaufman or Steve McQueen how that quackery worked for them. Both Hollywood legends sought controversial cancer treatments when they were in the latter stages of the disease. I understand desperate times call for desperate measures, and if I was dying from The Cancer and all conventional treatments were ineffective and exhausted, then I would be open to try anything. But I wouldn't *start* with the holistic schmuck.

No one really knows for sure what causes The Cancer. The disease has been linked to a variety of causes ranging from chemicals to the sun. Here we will explore some of the possible causes.

The Machines

Possible causes of The Cancer have been linked to everything ranging from diet to microwaves to cell phone use. Technological advances have made us more dependent on the use of these gadgets that enhance our everyday lives, namely cell phones and laptops. Advances in medical science and the use of X-Rays, MRIs, sonograms, ultrasounds, etc., have saved countless lives and increased life expectancy.

What we know is that all of these machines emit some level of radiation. What we don't know is how much radiation exposure is unsafe. Radiation is a hot topic as a cause of cancer. Just ask those poor people in Hiroshima.

It wasn't too long ago that I was a kid and the microwave (or new science ovens) came out. I remember my parents running into the next room like radiologists taking an X-Ray every time they were "nuking" something. More than once I was yanked out of the kitchen by my shirt collar if I got too close to the microwave oven while my mother was cooking.

> "Victor, do you want to get The Cancer?" my mother would say.
>
> "How is the microwave oven going to give me The Cancer?" I would ask.
>
> "I don't know how, but it could, what am I a scientist? Now go set the table for dinner".

It's pretty amazing that my mother was convinced the microwave oven could give you The Cancer, but it didn't stop her from cooking our dinner with it! My mother also said sitting too close to the color TV that sat in a wooden cabinet the size of a cruise ship would make me go blind. So they weren't right about everything, but I do wear glasses now.

The cell phone is a wonderful invention, isn't it? I mean who would have thought a machine that can keep you in constant contact with friends and family and help you manage your business more efficiently could possibly be dangerous to your health?

Well think back about twenty years ago when the first cell phones came out. Remember what they looked like? They looked like Geiger counters and were basically a large battery encased in a small suitcase. The receiver snapped off and attached to a cord that led to the battery. At the time we were all amazed at what they could do. To me it looked like something out of "Back to the Future". But I think we've lost sight of the fact that when you have a large hot battery next to your head sending radio waves and God knows what else through your skull, you just might be in danger.

Today's cell phones are small enough to fit in the palm of your hand and they perform many functions. Who would have thought such a thing could be possible? Maybe the bearded weirdo Nostradamus, but that is about it. But did anyone stop to think that to perform all these functions and store all this mega data, the device had to be more powerful, possibly sending even more radio waves through your brain?

Four G, five G and God knows what they will be up to by the time this book goes to print, the amount of bells and whistles cell phones have is amazing. But does it come with a cost to your health?

One of my best friends had a baseball sized tumor removed from his head. He believes the tumor was a result of all the hours he spent using his cell phone for work. He won't use a cell phone anymore, and if someone is using one near him he runs the hell out of the room. Who can blame him? Who would have thought a device that makes your life easier could also be causing tumors in your brain?

How about where you carry your cell phone when you're not using it? It's harmless right? Not so fast, just because it's not pressed against your brain does not necessarily mean you're not being exposed to some level of radiation. A cell phone still emits radiation whenever it's on. It is up to you where you keep it when it's not in use.

Women for the most part have it easy, they carry their cell phone in their handbag or teenage girls have them sticking out of their asses. Now for men, it gets a little tricky because there is no stylish way to carry a cell phone. There are three ways a man can carry a cell phone and none of them are good.

1. You can look like a douche bag and wear it clipped on to your belt. I'm sorry but anything affixed to your belt (with the exception of a gun holster) makes you look like a dick. Engineers, accountants, guys who frequent Star Trek conventions… you know who I'm talking about here. Walking around with a square device on your belt makes you look like, well, a square.

2. If the registered sex offender look is what you're going for, then by all means carry your cell phone in a fanny pack around your waist. While waiting outside a store in the mall, people will stare at your crotch thinking one thing: You have candy and condoms in your fanny pack and you're looking to steal a child. Never would anyone imagine your wife was inside OshKosh B'Gosh buying children's clothes while you waited outside sipping a Starbucks coffee, wearing your fanny pack and mom jeans.
3. Now if you're not interested in having children, and you're not afraid of testicular cancer, the more conventional method is to keep your cell phone inside your front pocket, right up against your balls. A roasted testicle is a hell of a price to pay for vanity. Fashion-wise, it's the lesser of 3 evils, although one would have to be blind to ignore the fact that there is a 4 inch square imprint in your crotch.

If you really have balls and want to throw caution to the wind, how about going for the cyborg look by plugging a Bluetooth device inside your head portal? How fucking busy or lazy can you be that you have to have a phone plugged into your ear canal?

Unless you're a quadriplegic, is lifting a cell phone to your head taking that much out of you? Besides the direct radiation going through your head, how about hearing loss? You don't have to be an audiologist to realize anything stuck inside your ear canal piping in sound is going to cause some form of hearing loss. If you're wearing a Bluetooth device screwed into your head, the question begs to be asked… Are you that dependent on your cellphone that you are willing to look like a total douchebag?

But why worry about a small insignificant cell phone when you have Wifi at home? Now you can sit in the privacy of your own home or overpriced coffee house sipping a tai chi latte or whatever it's called, while getting penetrated by high speed broadband radio waves, providing lightning fast wireless service to your phone, computer, or wireless printer that never seems to work. Think of it as getting a continuous MRI in the comfort of your home.

Trusting Men with White Teeth

We make conscious or sometimes unconscious decisions to expose ourselves to radiation, therefore possibly increasing our risk to The Cancer. It wasn't too long ago when we lived in a simpler world that didn't revolve around cell phones or electronic devices. Nowadays we cannot seem to live without our gadgets to entertain ourselves. We make the assumption that these devices are perfectly safe because they are sold legally in stores on the open market. So are six-thousand-calorie processed frozen pizzas, or turkey fryers whose directions are often ignored resulting in a hillbilly's deck burning to the ground.

We also make the assumption that going to our dentist twice a year is safe. But what if your dentist, whom you trust with your teeth, was exposing you to unnecessary radiation for profit?

Every dentist recommends you go in for a checkup twice a year, right? So why then does your dentist insist on X-raying your head every year to look for a possible cavity? A cavity sucks and is painful but it's not going to kill you. Even if your cavity is the size of a pothole, you can get a root canal and fake tooth that will never go bad put in. So the question begs to be asked, why does your dentist behave like an over aggressive TSA agent trying to locate an explosive device secreted in your mouth?

While you're lying helplessly in a dentist chair, your dental technician points a machine resembling a futuristic laser to your head. In reality it looks like a ray gun that a James Bond nemesis would use to kill him. The dental tech assures you the X-rays are perfectly safe as she throws a fifty pound lead bomb blanket over your crotch and proceeds to run out of the room like she owes you money.

"It's only a small amount of radiation" she yells from around the wall, as the drool rolls out of your mouth like a stroke victim's. Clenching an electronic sensor that resembles a Gitmo torture device inside your jaw, you hear a high pitch sound you hope isn't shortening your life.

Or you might have a more modern dentist like mine, who uses what looks like a state trooper's radar gun. I had to bite on what looked and tasted like a cell phone charger while the dental tech pointed a Jugs Radar Gun to my head monitoring traffic speed.

Unless you live in a cave, you are constantly bombarded with information telling you to take care of your teeth. Toothpaste, dental floss, and mouthwash commercials are on TV every fifteen minutes. Your supermarket and drugstore have at least a half aisle dedicated to keeping you out of a dentist's office. Supersonic battery powered toothbrushes do the brushing for you, saving you from "The Carpal Tunnel Syndrome".

For Christ sake, they put fluoride in the water whether we want it or not to save us from cavities. An aggressive dentist, like a short waiter, is not to be trusted.

So why does your dentist act as if a cavity is The Cancer and insists on taking X-rays of your mouth every year?

In my opinion it boils down to dollars and cents. To give you a comparative example of what I'm talking about, let's take a visit to your car dealership's service department.

When you buy a new car from a dealership, you usually get a 3 year/ 36,000 mile warranty. As a loyal customer, you bring your vehicle in for oil changes and maintenance at every recommended interval during the warranty period.

Watch what happens when you go in for an oil change and tire rotation after your 36,000 mile warranty expires. You took off from work today to run some errands and get your car serviced at your friendly neighborhood dealership service center. You love your car and baby the shit out of it. Garage kept, you only use premium gasoline and top grade synthetic oil at every 3,000 mile oil change. You arrive at the dealership and are greeted by the service manager who wears a shit-eating grin and treats you like a lifelong friend. Dressed in Khakis and a company polo shirt, he takes down your information and escorts you into the waiting room, making you feel like you don't have a care in the world.

After about an hour of sitting in the cozy waiting room listening to Barry Manilow and sipping a powdered cappuccino that's going to give you the runs, the service manager walks in. Mr. Khakis now carries a clipboard and grim face and sits down next to you. Looking like a doctor about to give you grave news, he struggles to find the words. Just before he opens his mouth you're thinking to yourself, "what could be wrong with my car?" and "I think that cappuccino has given me diarrhea!"

He fights through his emotions and finds the courage to give you the bad news. He proceeds to give you some bullshit story about carbon buildup or how sludge has suddenly appeared inside your engine or fuel injectors. It's really bad and if not addressed soon, the long term health and performance of your car will suffer a painful horrible death. You're in shock and didn't see this coming. Mr. Khakis has now fucked up your day.

Have no fear though because this dealership has the treatment for the mysterious sludge and/or carbon build up. For a mere $180 per treatment, Mr. Khakis is going to save your vehicle and make it as good as new!

I would have loved to have seen Mr. Khakis try this con on my father when I was a kid. He would have told him to shove the carbon buildup right up his ass.

As you sit there digesting the terrible news and holding off the runs, your common sense light should begin to kick in. You purchased your vehicle from this dealership. You bring it here for oil changes and service just as the manufacturer recommends. You buy your fuel from a reputable gas station and you don't drive like an asshole, racing around or revving the engine like a 17 year old with his first car.

You were just here three months ago when your car was under warranty and this khaki wearing jerkoff told you that your vehicle was in tip top shape. As a matter of fact, he couldn't get you out of there fast enough last time. Of course there was nothing wrong with your car 3,000 miles ago because it was still under warranty.

I'll bet car dealership mechanics are told to ignore anything wrong with a vehicle when it's under warranty. Unfortunately it's up to you to find what's wrong with your car and bring it to their attention when it is under warranty. Once the warranty expires, they take it upon themselves to start inventing problems.

Not more than 20 minutes earlier the preowned sales manager, wearing a Mr. Rogers kid snatcher sweater interrupted you sipping your laxative. He congratulated you on how well you were taking care of your vehicle. He even made an offer to buy it back from you because of the wonderful condition it was in. You're getting mixed signals. You have entered the twilight zone.

"Don't these two assholes talk to each other?" you ask yourself. I mean they work for the same company in the same fucking building. On one hand you have Mr. Rogers with his phony folksy tone buttering you up, trying to buy your car back with a lowball offer. On the other hand you have Mr. Khakis telling you your car's engine will seize unless you get this new recommended treatment you've never heard of before, practically making it seem as if your car is on its death bed. How could this happen all of a sudden? The reason is money. Now tell Mr. Khakis to go fuck himself and locate a toilet immediately.

If you're over 40, you can think back to a time when vehicles were not made to last. When I was a teenager, my friends and I were constantly replacing radiators, alternators, and starters every year to keep our cars running. My first new car was a 1987 Hyundai that basically fell apart after 30,000 miles. Today's vehicles and parts are designed to last much longer.

Most vehicles have platinum spark plugs rated up to 100,000 miles and can go up to 10,000 miles between oil changes. The parts and systems last longer in today's vehicles, meaning you visit your mechanic less and less. That's great isn't it? I mean today's vehicles cost more, but you're getting a better product, right?

If technology has made the motor vehicle a better product, therefore requiring less maintenance, how are the dealerships going to recoup the loss of revenue they were used to from servicing and replacing the old, inferior parts that no longer exist?

Well if you think the car dealership and dentist are going to take this lost revenue via technology lying down, you've got another thing coming.

The fact is the guy in the khakis, and your dentist for that matter, are telling you bullshit stories.

Auto manufacturers have gotten creative, designing vehicles to be computerized so you basically cannot work on them anymore. You have to plug them into a computer to find the source of any problem. Unless you're in the business of fixing cars, you're not going to spend a couple of thousand dollars on a computer to plug your car into.

I once changed the headlight bulb on my Nissan. I felt like a vascular surgeon performing open heart surgery as I snaked my hand through a maze of metal and plastic.

Now apply my twisted logic to your dentist who recommends X-raying your head every year. You know your mouth. You brush, floss, and for the most part, are the only one who puts anything in it. How much could have changed in a year since the last time you had an X-ray? Unless you are chewing glass or flossing with barbwire, what could have happened?

What's the worst case scenario if you don't get your yearly X-ray? Let's say two months after you blow off your X-ray, you get a toothache. Well now you know you have a problem. Now it's time to stand tall before the man and eat some humble pie, the kind of pie that won't cause a cavity.

Go back to your dentist, hat in hand, bend the knees, and genuflect. Let him take the X-rays of your mouth while he pisses in your ear about how this could have been prevented two months earlier, when you did not heed his professional opinion. Let him puff out his chest and brow beat you, while you moan in agonizing pain lying helplessly in his chair.

He's a DDS and has it designated on his license plates to prove it, bitch! For God's sake, you best show some respect and listen to him next time!

My first trip to my high tech dentist was an experience. The questionnaire I filled out had more questions than the loan application to purchase my house. Every person in the place wore a wireless headset so they could communicate like the secret service moving the president through a building.

While lying in his chair like a stiff at a funeral parlor, he handed me a mirror and asked me to look at myself. He then asked, "If there was anything I could change for you, what would it be?"

I told him my wish was to not lie in his chair anymore. He tried selling me everything from cleaning my gums with a laser to braces. I told him, "I'm almost fifty and couldn't model socks, why would I want braces?"

"Well you want to look good, don't you?" he had the balls to ask.

I am going to go out on a limb here and say our pal the dentist is no longer getting the same bang for his buck. He isn't making the same money he used to, because advances in dental science have made the occurrence of a cavity less and less. So like the guy in khakis at the car dealership, he had to reinvent himself with something to fill the void of lost income.

Unlike Mr. Khakis who probably lives check to check, the dentist is eyeing new Callaway golf clubs while watching his country club fees go up every year.

That's their problem not yours, so why chance the exposure of unnecessary radiation? But what do we do? We go in like sheep and let them do what they want because they have a framed piece of paper on their wall telling us they are dentists.

You know what else dentists have on their walls? Dental porn. Posters of gorgeous women with beautiful smiles or framed teeth cartoons holding toothbrushes telling us to floss. So why are we taking these people so seriously?

What they should also have on their wall is something telling you how much radiation you are going to be exposed to per X-ray session.

When you buy any prepackaged edible at your supermarket, there's a label telling you the calories, nutritional value, and ingredients that you're about to consume. Your cashier does not require you to wear a lead vest nor does she hide beneath the counter as your items are scanned through checkout.

So is it too much to ask to get a straight answer on whether or not your annual X-ray is necessary, and if so, how much radiation you are actually exposed to and at what risk?

As I'm lecturing you about the possible dangers of radio, micro, and gamma rays, I'm writing on a laptop the size of a Papa John's pizza sitting atop my balls. I'm guessing a warm machine which also sends radio waves isn't the best thing to be sitting on top of your crotch.

If you want to be sterile, be my guest, otherwise at least put a pillow over your crotch while using your laptop. I'm just putting it out there.

Death by Vanity a.k.a. "The Skin Cancer" or The Melanoma

Here's some breaking scientific news: the sun can kill you. Yes, the sun, or for those of you listening in Spanish via audiobook, "El Sol". Skin cancer is the most common form of cancer in both men and women, although if you use common sense, your chances of getting it are pretty slim.

I remember when I was a teen, I used baby oil and a mirror to enhance a dark tan. Those days are over and it's pretty common knowledge that too much sun is bad for you. Not only can too much sun kill you, it will make you look like shit before it finishes you off.

If you want your skin to look like a Rawlings baseball glove or the Indian who cried because his river got polluted, be my guest. It boils down to folks who want to look good and take shortcuts to get there at the expense of their health. I would rather put Hellmann's mayonnaise sunblock on my skin than get the dreaded melanoma. Knowing what I know now, I cringe while thinking back to how stupid I was as a teen, exposing myself to countless hours, unprotected in the sun.

Back in the 1970s my parents had never heard of sunblock. In the summer, we would drive on family vacations and my father, who didn't believe in air conditioning, would hang his pale Irish arm out of the window for hours at a time. By about the second day, the poor guy had red dots (or what we now know is sun poisoning) all over his left arm. To this day I'm amazed he didn't develop skin cancer after all those hours of sun exposure.

The sun can be good for you in small doses, but like with sex, you really should use protection. Sunlight in moderation provides us with vitamin D and is proven to keep us in a good mood. Ask all those depressed people who don't see the sun very often in Alaska or Seattle.

In this day and age with all the products available, there really is no reason why you should have too much unprotected exposure to the sun. You can even go in the water now without worrying about your sunblock washing off. If you're not into having cold slimy lotions applied to your body, you can go "old skool" and wear a hat, or one of those newly invented long sleeve shirts to protect your epidermis!

If you're impatient and can't wait for a sunny day, here's another sure fire way to increase your chance of developing skin cancer; the tanning bed. I know I'm lecturing about shortcuts again, but it's true. When you take shortcuts with common sense, you run the risk of shortening your life.

In a perfect world, a tanning bed would be used under a doctor's, or at the very least, a registered nurse's supervision, to limit your ultraviolet ray exposure. A tanning bed would be calibrated and serviced at regular intervals by medical professionals.

Unfortunately in the real world, you get an airhead hairstylist who instead of monitoring your time in a tanning bed, is rocking out to Pandora on her iPhone. Like at a self-service car wash, you pay by the minute so you can lay in a tanning bed for as long as you want, exposing yourself to unnecessary ultraviolet rays.

When you sit on a toilet seat in a public bathroom, you hope they have the paper asshole horseshoe punch out lining to protect your ass from touching the toilet seat. So riddle me this… why on earth would you lay your entire almost naked, or if you're European, totally naked body on a surface that is used by the public?

Even a whorehouse changes the sheets once in a while. I know, ultraviolet light is supposed to kill germs, but still. Go ahead, take the easy way out and lay in that filthy thing. You'll probably get a nice case of the crabs or dancing dandruff head lice while simultaneously killing off your skin cells.

What amazes me is that here in Florida, the sun capital of the United States, people still use tanning beds. All you have to do is sit in your backyard, or go for a walk in a tee shirt and a pair of shorts for twenty minutes to get some color. But in our vain society, we want instant gratification. You really don't have twenty minutes for a walk? It's going to take the moron at the tanning salon twenty minutes just to run your credit card.

Now if the sun or tanning bed take too much time and you still want color, a spray on tan is another sure fire way to risk your health. If you want to look like Goldfinger's ex-girlfriend, you can go the Earl Schieb route and get yourself bronzed like baby shoes.

Earl Schieb made millions of dollars painting any car, any color at discount prices. You could spot a cheap Earl Scheib paint job from a mile away. I know, because as a kid I went there twice with my shitbox car for paint jobs. A cheap paint job, like a spray on tan, just doesn't look right.

You can choose from a wide variety of color skin tones at your spray tan facility for a lot less than Earl Scheib's $99.95 special. Skin tones range from Copper Penny, Tan Mom, or Mandingo, transforming you into a chocolate Easter rabbit.

If you have the balls, go walk the beach after your spray tan and watch as people stare at you in horror. Just because they are pointing and laughing at you, does not change the fact you're a bronzed god, right?

Don't forget to close your mouth during your spraying session or your brown teeth may give it away. If that does happen, your dentist will happily bleach your teeth, giving you a ridiculous contrast of bronzed skin and fluorescent white teeth. Try not to breathe while your tan tech professional, most likely a high school dropout with a slight methamphetamine problem, sprays you from head to toe like a Buick, with a supposedly safe substance that makes your skin look like a piece of mahogany.

I don't care what anybody says, inhaling tanning spray into your lungs cannot be good for you. The same goes for being covered with a dye that covers ninety percent of your pores.

You're better off looking like an albino than tempting the sun or playing around with artificial light or spray dyes just to look good. I'm also guessing you're going to spend a lot of money on laundry detergent when your fake tan rubs onto your clothes and bedding.

Most of us will get moles, freckles, or skin tags in our lifetime because Father Time is not kind to our skin. It sucks to get old but it's a reality of life. Most of the time, we either ignore them or never even notice them. Quoting my dermatologist, "Your skin is a birthday cake, the older we get, the more candles we receive".

Skin cancer, if detected early, is one of the most survivable cancers. It usually sits right out in the open, under our very noses daring us to find it. If it turns into The Melanoma, it quickly becomes one of the most deadly forms of cancer. What makes melanoma so deadly is that it spreads through your blood into your organs, making it very difficult to treat.

After you read this, I want you to make an appointment with a dermatologist. They know the difference between a mole and The Melanoma.

Like most of us, I don't like going to the doctor. But in my opinion, of all the doctors you're going to see in your lifetime, the dermatologist is the least intrusive. You put on a gown and sit on a table while he examines your skin under a bright light. If he sees something he doesn't like, he numbs the area and slices off a very small portion of skin with what looks like a cheese wire slicer and sends the sample off to a lab.

The whole procedure takes 2 minutes and is painless. The only painful part of the visit is the copayment. You won't make it past the bossy pear shaped nurse without her grabbing you, so just pay her and be on your way.

And now a list of DOs and DON'Ts for the "pigmentally challenged":

DOs:

- 20 minute walk in the sun (Irish & Germans, limit it to 5 minute walk)
- If you're bald, wear a hat. Plugs or comb over may work too.

- Wear jeans and long sleeve shirts if you have red hair or if your last name begins with an O'

DON'Ts:

- Attend beach bar wet T shirt contest longer than 1 hour without sunblock
- Consume more than 3 Long Island Iced Teas outdoors, or anywhere ever!
- Pick at or remove skin tags

If you want to look like an alligator bag or a wooden Indian in a cigar store, be my guest; just don't say you weren't warned. If it's that important to die for a Coppertone tan, there's no helping you.

Cancer by Habit

Now if you've been in a cave for the last thirty years and haven't heard the rumor that smoking will kill you, just tear the pages out of this book and wipe your ass with it because there is no helping you. How anyone can think that inhaling any kind of smoke into your lungs could be good for you is beyond me. By now we all have seen the commercials showing some poor bastard, who after years of smoking, is a mess. There's the guy in the shower with a hole in his throat, or the former homecoming queen speaking through a cancer kazoo. I don't know about you, but to me these convey pretty vivid images of the dangers of smoking.

Gone are the days when tobacco companies could pull the wool over the eyes of the so called naive public by having doctors performing cigarette commercials. The Marlboro Man had his last rodeo over twenty years ago, and for the most part, government has made smoking quasi illegal. When was the last time you saw a cigarette commercial on television?

You can't smoke in most restaurants, bars, or outdoor events. I remember the good ol' days when you could though. After spending the evening at a bar or restaurant, the next day your hair and clothes had a stale smoke smell and your voice was raw.

Back when I was a cop, I worked with two guys who were chain smokers. One time I came down with a bad chest cold and sore throat and visited the doctor.

"Vic, you really should stop smoking, you sound terrible and your throat is raw", the doctor warned.

"I've never smoked in my life", I replied. After explaining to the doctor that I was trapped all day in a car with two guys who smoked like chimneys, the doctor told me, "Get as far away from that car as you can, it's going to affect your health in the long run".

He didn't have to tell me twice and I found another couple of guys to work with.

Slowly but surely, public opinion has changed in regards to smoking. People still smoke, but for the most part not in the public domain. It's almost like smoking has become an underground vice like alcohol during the prohibition era. What used to be considered sexy or stylish is now called a filthy habit.

You have to be over 18 years old to purchase tobacco, and good luck finding an establishment that will allow you to light up. If you had the balls to light up a cigarette near children today, mothers would shield their kids like you threw anthrax on them. You would be lectured on the dangers of secondhand smoke and how it could impact their kids' development.

I know this all too well because my dad blew cigarette smoke into my crib, and I never made it to six feet tall, but I did go on to greatness by writing this informative book.

Class action lawsuits and settlements have driven the price of cigarettes through the roof. You would think that when the price of tobacco went up, people would have stopped smoking. The only thing the lawsuits and government fines did was hit the smokers (or victims) in the pocket.

It drove smokers into inventive ways to find places to smoke and obtain cheap cigarettes. Now smokers buy cigarettes online or purchase cartons of untaxed cigarettes from Indian reservations. If getting my hands on something is a pain in the ass and too expensive, it's not worth it for me.

Remember my father, the guy who didn't believe in air conditioning and got sun poisoning on family vacations? He smoked about four packs of Lucky (or unlucky for him) Strikes a day.

As I sat crammed behind him in our two door Datsun B210, he would smoke away, flicking his ashes and lit cigarette butts out the window, meaning they would inevitably fly back into my head in the back seat. He burned many of my t shirts and singed my head a few times. That was more than enough of a reason for me not to take up smoking. But if you want to shorten your life, have brown teeth and yellow fingers, by all means light up.

My father quit smoking when he was 47 years old and we were all proud of him. Years of hearing him wake up in the morning coughing up green phlegm were over.

Twenty years later, at 68 years old he developed double pneumonia and never recovered. The doctors told me his lungs were so badly damaged after 30 years of smoking there wasn't much they could do for him. He had defeated his addiction but the damage was done. His past had unfortunately come back to haunt him.

I was at the hospital day and night as he lay in an induced coma with almost pure oxygen pumped into his scarred lungs, keeping him alive. A few times doctors woke him just to make sure his brain was still alive. I could tell by the look in his face he was suffering and in great pain. My father was a great guy who suffered a terrible and avoidable death because of smoking.

If you're a smoker and reading this, I hope I am scaring the shit out of you. Please do yourself a favor and stop smoking before it's too late.

Another interesting and sexy way to get nicotine into your body is to chew it. Nothing is more attractive than a guy or gal spitting out a cheek full of tobacco juice. You don't see spittoons anymore, so why do people still think chewing tobacco is fashionable?

I understand in the Wild West people didn't know any better, but times have changed. People don't ride horses to bars anymore nor do they rustle cattle. So why would you insist on this dangerous and disgusting habit?

I've never kissed anyone who chewed tobacco but I cannot imagine it being fun. They say kissing a smoker is like kissing an ashtray. So by that rationale, is kissing a tobacco chewer like kissing a spittoon? If tobacco is bad for your lungs, why would you think it's good for your mouth? Mouth, tongue, and cheek cancers have all been attributed to chewing tobacco. So if you want your lower jaw to fall off some day, keep chewing away.

Too Legit to Quit

People will always find a way to rationalize something that isn't good for them. We create a facade showing we are attempting to stop or curb a bad habit, though not cutting it out completely.

We try to convince ourselves or anyone else who will listen that by altering a bad habit, it isn't as bad as being all in.

I worked with a guy who was a very heavy smoker for many years. On top of his smoking problem, he had another; he had told his wife he had quit smoking years ago. Every day before he left work, he would brush his teeth for twenty minutes followed by mouthwash. On his hour commute home to the suburbs, he would suck on Altoid after Altoid. He explained to his wife that his hair and clothes smelled like cigarette smoke as a result of the "other" smokers in the office.

The ruse worked for a while, until he had to take a physical for a life insurance policy. He gave up smoking for about 90 days to clear out his system. After he had his policy approved, it was business as usual, and he couldn't wait to puff away.

When we were kids, my dad tried a few times to kick smoking. His weight would balloon up when he quit and he would become quite irritable. Even as kids we figured out he didn't have the usual amount of patience he would have when he was smoking. We just tried to stay out of his way and went to our mother to sort out any problems until he was able to kick the habit for good.

We all know how hard it is to stop smoking because nicotine is a very addictive substance. Go to any drugstore and you will find a variety of products made to help you stop smoking. Nicotine gums, patches or enemas are all the equivalent of methadone. Think about it, you're still getting the nicotine in your body, you're just not absorbing it through your lungs. You're still going to crave it and become edgy when you don't get your fix.

In my opinion, to quit cigarette smoking is quite similar to kicking a heroin habit. A heroin addict will go through withdrawal and become physically ill (dope sick) unless they get heroin into their system. The supposed safe substitute to heroin is the drug methadone, which is supposed to wean addicts off heroin, but it seldom works.

Methadone will stop the physical sickness of heroin withdrawal, but does absolutely nothing to curb the insatiable craving of heroin. I know as I had a whole career of arresting and babysitting heroin addicts.

Going back to what I said earlier about people altering bad habits, let's talk about the supposedly safe alternative to cigarette smoking: the vapor E-cigarette. The E-cigarette has become the new chic way to enjoy nicotine.

You go out and buy the new electronic cigarette cartridges to supposedly wean you off your nicotine habit. It's not as bad, right? I mean you're not inhaling cigarette smoke, you're just inhaling a warm liquid vapor of nicotine. You're not blowing smoke on anyone and it's supposedly odorless.

E-cigarette lounges are popping up all over the place, offering various flavored vapor cartridges that snap into your battery powered puffing device. You can sit in a dim lit opium den environment with other vapor inhalers, mimicking lightning bugs on a summer evening every time you take a drag.

These things look just like crack pipes to me. Have you ever heard a crack head's voice? After years of puffing away on the glass dick, you can use a crack head's voice to sand your floors.

Ten years from now when people start developing all sorts of lung ailments, ambulance chasing attorneys will air commercials. "Have you been the victim of an E-cigarette?"

How can this be? Who would have thought that inhaling an addictive hot vapor into your lungs would cause health problems? The last time I looked, the inside of your lungs is a dark, moist, warm place that runs best on clean air. So why would you inhale anything else into them? If earning the nickname "scorch" doesn't bother you, by all means keep puffing away.

Or you can go see your doctor, who can prescribe one of those wonder drugs to help kick your smoking habit. Why try kicking your habit cold turkey when you can take a pill? It's medically proven safe and approved by the FDA, right? A doctor prescribed it, so what could go wrong?

Well, side effects may include nightmares, running into traffic while naked, and starting fires. So what if the new anti-smoking drug has side effects that mimic a bad acid trip? After picking up your prescription you can go to a Phish concert and trip out legally.

Alcohol

Another fun way to get The Cancer and shorten your life is by drinking too much alcohol. Unlike cigarettes, alcohol does not carry a dirty stigma with it. Unless you're living in a dry county in the Bible Belt or hanging with a bunch of Baptists, having a drink is socially acceptable. Doctors actually advocate the health benefits of having a glass of wine or a beer. And who doesn't like happy hour?

The problem with alcohol is when people go off the reservation and drink too much, too often. The effects of long term alcohol abuse are stunning. Liver, kidney, and colon cancer, along with Alzheimer's have all been attributed to excessive alcohol consumption. Alcohol, like tobacco, can cause you to age prematurely by wreaking havoc on your internal organs and skin. The shakes, gin blossoms, and liver spots are all terrible side effects of alcoholism.

Drinking too much alcohol can also influence you to make bad decisions. So how do you know when you are crossing the line between safety and stupidity with your alcohol consumption? If you have ever found yourself in one of these situations, you may be an alcoholic.

- Pissing on a mailbox with car keys in hand, unable to locate where you parked your car.
- Attempting to obtain the phone number of some soup head who's fallen off her barstool more than once in twenty minutes.
- Vomiting into a strange toilet that has more rings than Saturn.
- Waking up with a headache, trying to comprehend what you said or did the night before.
- A 7am wakeup call from the police, who would like to talk to you about something that happened the previous evening.
- Waking up to find a commingling of cash and receipts in your pockets from places you don't remember visiting.
- Waking up to find you are pissing into a chair at an Indian gaming casino.
- Drinking a full bottle of wine while home alone watching infomercials or QVC.
- Waking up to find your so-called friends have posted photos of you on Facebook, showing your mouth touching something it shouldn't have touched.
- Waking up to find those same so-called friends (what's it going to take to stay away from them?) have shaved off one of your eyebrows.

You don't have to be a Mensa member to know drinking too much alcohol is bad for your health and enables you to make poor decisions which will later embarrass the crap out of you.

If you don't believe me, here is a fun way to see what will happen to you if you drink too much. Go to your local dive bar, VFW, Elk or Moose Lodge, and order one of their warm, flat, premium tap beers. The tap lines have not been cleaned in years, making Old Milwaukee and Pabst Blue Ribbon indistinguishable, but will ensure a terrible hangover the following day.

While sipping your headache in a cup, enjoy the aroma of aged farts coming from other patrons and the stench of mold coming from behind the bathroom walls. Don't forget to visit the men's room, where you can play global warming, pretending to melt the polar ice caps by pissing on the stale ice that's been dumped into the urinals.

Eavesdrop on other drunks telling stories that make Billy Joel's "Piano Man" sound like an uplifting song.

My point is if any of this sounds vaguely familiar to you, you are drinking too much and should slow down or seek professional help, if you need it.

I am not a teetotaler and enjoy my wine and beer, but like anything else, with the exception of hot yoga, too much of anything is usually not good for you.

The colon cancer

When I was in my early twenties, I drove my father to a colonoscopy procedure. I was naive and really had no idea what the procedure entailed. During the ride, my father began explaining it to me, putting me in shock.

"You mean they are going to shove a pipe up your ass to look around?!" I asked.

"Not a pipe jerkoff, a camera" my dad explained.

I hung around the waiting room while he received his colonoscopy. When he came out about an hour later, he was in a fog from the anesthesia. On the ride home he explained they had removed a couple of polyps and sent them off to the lab for analysis.

"Wait, that pipe has scissors to snip stuff in your ass?" I asked.

"Something like that and I cannot believe I raised a moron" my father replied as he farted uncontrollably all the way home.

The uncontrollable farting was funny, but the procedure my dad had just endured scared the shit out of me. The thought of getting knocked out and having a guy snake a cable up my ass, taking pictures and making alterations in there did not sit well with me. I pictured a bunch of people standing over me, laughing at what my asshole looks like.

I took a deep breath and relaxed because I was twenty years old and getting a colonoscopy (or "The Pipe" as my friends called it) was light years away. The way I figured, by the time I was fifty, they will have a better method of looking up my ass than to snake a cable with scissors up in there.

What Goes around Comes Around: "The Pipe", A Real Pain in the Ass

As you have already guessed, not much has changed in ass exploration since the day I took my dad in for his colonoscopy over thirty years ago. A couple of years ago, my stomach was bothering me and I went to a gastroenterologist to figure out what was wrong. As he was asking me questions about my diet, all I could think about was," is this guy going to recommend 'The Pipe'?"

"Victor, I really would have to look around your gastrointestinal tract to figure out what is giving you this pain", Dr. Pipe said. "Plus you're almost fifty and you really should be screened for 'The colon cancer', so I highly recommend you get a colonoscopy", he said.

Like a child, for twenty minutes I tried to talk my way out of it.

Finally he said "Victor, what are you so scared of?"

I explained my fear of medical procedures. "Can I do the colonoscopy awake?" I asked.

"Why would you want to do that?"

"If somebody yells 'fire' during the procedure, I can pull the cable out of my ass and run out the door" I said.

Finally I came clean and explained my fear of anesthesia and he agreed to do the procedure while I was awake.

The day of the procedure, I went to the clinic only to find out my doctor owns the place, who would have thought? The nurse at the receiving desk photocopied my insurance card and asked me if I have a living will. I told her no but offered to leave everything to her in the event I die with a cable in my ass. She didn't laugh, and yes, she was pear shaped.

In the prep room, I put on a gown and was greeted by another nurse. She began to rub alcohol on my arm telling me this was for my anesthesia.

"I told the nurse up front I don't want anesthesia" I said. She said ok and left the room.

Two minutes later, this bald guy in scrubs walks into the room. "Hi, I am your anesthesiologist".

I jumped off the gurney. "Get this fucking guy out of here!" I said. "No God damn anesthesia!" I yelled.

The anesthesiologist didn't miss a beat and said "I'm going to lunch" and turned around and left. I was then wheeled into another room on a gurney like a corpse.

My poor girlfriend, who had been sitting in the waiting room, heard the entire ruckus. She later told me, "I knew it was you. When you went back there, I gave it fifty-fifty odds you might come running out of there in your gown".

Awaiting me was my gastroenterologist and 2 nurses, one of whom resembled the rock star, Meatloaf. There was a large flat screen TV on the wall and I was turned on my side. The doctor lubed up the cable with KY jelly like he was Caligula.

"You ready Victor?" he asked.

"Let's go, snake charmer", I replied, and the fun began. "I want to go on record here and note that other than my mother putting a thermometer up there, or the occasional doctor's finger, I have never had anything stuck in my ass".

It didn't hurt but it was sure uncomfortable as I watched my colon in high definition on the Jumbotron.

As he slid up memory lane, it amazed me what my insides looked like. The pink slimy walls of my intestines reminded me of looking down somebody's throat. Every now and then, he had to blow air up my ass so that the cable could slide through easier. That cable is amazing. It takes photos, blows air up your ass, and slices and dices if necessary.

During the procedure, I made small talk with the doctor and asked a question that had haunted me.

"I took that super laxative last night to clean myself out" I said. "Do you ever get a fucking idiot who comes in for a colonoscopy right after he had a meatball hero?"

The entire staff began to laugh, when I realized they should be more concerned with my colon than my standup routine.

"All the time" the doctor replied.

The only time it really hurt was on the cable's way out when the doctor had to make a U-turn around my sigmoid colon cul de sac. Honestly, on a scale from 1-10, I would rate the pain about a 6. The whole thing took about twenty minutes. Everything went well, and like my dad had done almost thirty years earlier, I serenaded my girlfriend with a concerto of farts all the way home.

Here is the point of this embarrassing story. If I can do it, so can you. I'm the biggest pussy in the world when it comes to going to a doctor. How many people have died of colon cancer, a very treatable disease, because they were embarrassed to go for a screening?

We are lucky enough to live in a time when technology enables doctors to see what is going on inside our bodies. Think about all the guess work that went on before they had these cameras and procedures. Even if they were able to figure out you had colon cancer, they had to cut you open for an invasive surgery that many people did not survive.

Doctors recommend you get a colonoscopy when you hit fifty years old. The way I look at it, fifty is the perfect age to do something embarrassing like a colonoscopy. Come on, all the shit that has happened to you by the time you hit fifty, The Pipe is not a big deal. By the time you've hit fifty, you have been fired from at least one job, walked out of the bathroom with your fly open, or farted in front of a room full of people.

Today if the doctor locates a polyp, he snips it out and sends it off to the lab. If God forbid it's something more serious, they can begin a variety of treatments that greatly increase your odds of surviving. I know getting chemotherapy or radiation sucks, but the alternative is a lot worse.

So why take the chance with something that is basically avoidable? Be a man or woman for God's sake, and go get The Pipe!!

The Prostate Cancer: The Finger

Prostate cancer is the second leading cancer in men. 1 in 39 will die from it. 1 in 39, huh? That's almost the odds of winning at roulette. Still too high for me. But like colon cancer, it's very treatable if detected early.

It's not bad enough you have to get "The Pipe" every five years, we men get double banged. We get "The Finger" up our ass or the Digital rectal exam (DRE). I've had the exam and there is absolutely nothing digital or LED about it. The only thing remotely digital was when the doctor shoved his second digit up my crack.

I know women are going to call bullshit here, reminding men of the pain of childbirth, pap smears and Hiroshima, but I can only give firsthand accounts of my unfortunate experiences.

The prostate is a wonder gland for men, acting as a toll booth for the urethra that runs directly through it. When either sperm or urine pass through the prostate, it will squeeze giving you a wonderful ejaculation or a powerful piss stream that can chip a porcelain toilet. Everything is copasetic until you begin to age and your prostate decides it's time to bust balls and enlarge.

When the prostate (or toll taker) begins to push on the urethra, that's when the fun begins. Your sex life can go in the toilet and you can develop DDS, otherwise known as Dead Dick Syndrome. An enlarged prostate can also cause you to have to piss every thirty minutes, turning your once powerful stream into a drippy faucet wetting your shoes.

The test itself takes about 30 seconds from the time he puts on a glove, lubes up his finger, and bends you over the table. If you've never had anything up your ass before, it's going to feel weird and uncomfortable. The doctor's hand will slide up your ass like a sock puppet and you'll jump to your tippy toes praying for it to be over.

When he's finished, you're going to feel like a 20 dollar crack whore when he tells you to pull up your pants while you stand there with a slimy ass. He didn't even have the decency to hand me a towel on his way out the door. I almost wanted him to throw money at me and tell me to get the fuck out.

Visiting a urologist for a prostate cancer screening is definitely not a fun way to spend the afternoon, but it's not the end of the world. In addition to the finger, you should also get a PSA blood test to make sure everything is working ok. I know, who wants to go through all of this crap, but if you do the preventative maintenance, your chances of living a longer life increase significantly.

The Cancer is the wildcard of death. You can eat right, avoid carcinogens, and limit your sun intake. You can lead a clean life and live in the mountains breathing the freshest air, eating only organic food.

But the reality of cancer is nobody really knows what sets it in motion or how to stop it with utmost certainty. When someone supposedly beats cancer, they use the word remission. Meaning the possibility of cancer returning to the patient is higher than in someone who has never developed it. You should do what you can to avoid it, but in reality it's the luck of the draw. Try to eat healthy, avoid smoking and excessive alcohol consumption, and enjoy your life!

Chapter 3

Listen To Your Heart

The good old fashioned American heart attack is something that is unfortunately near and dear to my own heart. They usually strike without warning, and can be fatal. Like a bite from a venomous snake, you can survive if you realize what's happening and receive help in time.

Seeking medical treatment immediately and not blowing off the symptoms are key. It's a terrible shame how many people have died ignoring the warning signs. If you're experiencing symptoms of a heart attack, don't self-diagnose and chalk up your chest pain to the calzone you had for lunch or nothing a good fart couldn't cure. That's ridiculous. You're a plumber not a doctor, you wouldn't call the doctor to snake your toilet would you?

Call an ambulance or have someone drive you to the hospital and get yourself checked out. Provided the fact you're lucky enough to even get a warning sign and not croak where you stand.

It's too bad cemetery headstones don't list the cause of death and how old the person was when they died instead of forcing us to add the years. Maybe in the not too distant future, headstones will be interactive with a touch screen to view segments of a person's life, and will show how they died. After watching a couple of headstone videos of guys grabbing their chest and falling over in the front yard, you'd be hailing a cab to get a stress test.

But what happens if you go to the emergency room for chest pain and it turns out that nothing is wrong? Yes, it's going to cost you money for the ambulance ride and emergency room visit. Yes, you are going to wait forever, filling out forms while people cough on you. Yes, you are going to scare the shit out of your loved ones, provided you have any, who will say "It was only a matter of time before this happened" or "He's always been a hypochondriac", depending on your diagnosis. Yes, you may need a stent to clear a meatball out of your artery. And yes, it's going to be a pain in the ass dealing with your insurance company to recoup some of your money after it's all over. But do you want the other alternative?

You can roll the dice, ignore your chest pain, and opt not to go to the hospital. Save the money on the hospital visit and put it towards your upcoming funeral. Do it right and have an open bar with live music or a karaoke machine. Show your loved ones how much of a sport you were by treating them to some libations while you lie in a casket.

If you are reading this book, you more than likely live in the United States of America. Filthy rich Arab Sheiks come to our country at great expense to gain access to our doctors and facilities. We have the best medical care in the world.

It seems like every time we visit the doctor, there is a new drug, test or gadget to improve our lives. Children now have their temperature taken by a gadget that grazes their forehead, because the plastic tube that went into their ear was deemed too intrusive.

When I was a child, I used to get a glass rod shoved up my ass while my mother screamed at me not to clench or it would break in there. How's that for progress?

I would rather spend every dime I had to keep myself alive than leave a large bank account to my relatives to fight over after I was dead. People go into debt for the stupidest things.

I know some have gone into hock because of medical expenses, but that pales in comparison to what people spend their money on these days. If you don't believe me, stop by your local Costco or big box retailer some time and watch some 300 pound fat bastard who can barely move, sweating his balls off wheeling out a sixty inch flat screen TV instead of scheduling a stress test. They both probably cost about the same but the flat screen won't potentially save your life.

There is no better investment you can make than to use your money to keep yourself healthy and alive. I'm willing to put my money where my mouth is and if I sell enough copies of this book, I'm buying myself a hyperbaric chamber to sleep in. Hopefully it does wonders for my health, or I could just be known as the eccentric moron who sleeps in a hyperbaric chamber.

I was lucky enough to have all four of my grandparents alive until I was about seventeen. Unfortunately all four of them had heart problems and didn't do much about it. Just another ailment passed down from generation to generation, which I have to look forward to as I play the game of life.

My maternal grandparents had it the worst. Grandma had one of the first pacemakers installed and would tell anyone who would listen about the procedure. She was a large chested woman and if you got within 3 feet of her, she was going to show you the lump in her chest where the pacemaker was implanted, whether you wanted to see it or not. Come to think of it, her doctor had some pair of balls performing that surgery on her. She was very overweight and not the ideal patient for a relatively new procedure.

But like I said, when your doctor needs new golf clubs, why not give it a try. Off the boat from Europe, she had a flair for the dramatic and when she felt she wasn't getting enough attention, she would grab her chest and perform her best Fred G Sanford imitation, pleading with everyone in the room that this was it. It was tough on my parents who had to rely on their bullshit detector, having to differentiate between a Yugoslavian publicity stunt and a pending heart attack, when deciding whether or not to call an ambulance. Grandma did have heart problems, but more than once she checked herself into the hospital for an unnecessary tune up just for the attention.

Grandpa was the polar opposite and had to be dragged to the hospital. He wanted no part of the emergency room or doctors for that matter. You had to keep an eye on him because he would escape from the hospital and find his way home without telling hospital staff! More than once, my parents had to call the hospital to explain that my grandfather released himself on his own recognizance and was home safe.

My grandfather was a bartender who claimed he threw a drunken Ethel Mermen out of his bar in the 1940s or 1950s, after she smacked around a fellow patron. Grandpa was a low key guy who popped nitroglycerin pills like Tic-Tacs. He kept them in the medicine cabinet and if he felt faint, he would put one under his tongue like mescaline and let it dissolve. Once I slammed a door after he popped one of his pills. He said it felt like the top of his head had blown off. I guess grandpa was having a bad trip or something.

Grandpa had the open heart surgery in the 1970s and I can remember looking in amazement at the surgical scars on his chest which made him look like a hagstrom road map. Even as a child I thought to myself it looked painful.

It always seemed like at least one grandparent was in the hospital at any given time for some type of heart problem. For a kid, it's kind of traumatic having an ambulance show up to your house, strap your elderly grandparent to a stretcher, and cart him off to the hospital while he's arguing about not wanting to go. The funny thing is a couple of times the ambulance drivers would remember us from previous encounters.

I think I spent a third of my childhood at Westchester Square Hospital in the Bronx, visiting my grandparents. Back then, hospitals were not kid friendly. Slipping past the square badged security officer was like an episode of Mission Impossible.

The other option was to wait downstairs, bored out of my mind and getting on my poor father's last nerve, since he was tasked with keeping an eye on my brother and me while mom was visiting the patient upstairs.

Two of my grandparents smoked and all four had less than ideal diets. They never stopped smoking, nor did they alter their diets as they seemed content to accept their fates. It always seemed like they were cooking something delicious.

We lived with my mother's parents, and with my father being a butcher, I now realize it was a recipe for disaster. In the good ol' 1970s when red meat was good for you, my dad would bring it home literally by the trunkful.

Dad didn't make much money and worked for one of the supermarket chains. One of the perks, or so I then thought, was that he got free meat to bring home. One would think he would come through the door after work with a brown shopping bag full of steaks. Not my father, he wore his meat home like a bullet proof vest.

Every Thursday evening, my dad would come home and begin the ritual of taking off his sweatshirts one by one. He wore multiple to protect himself from the cold freezers he worked in. By about the third sweatshirt, you could see the meat vest;

packages of meat strapped to his chest with white adhesive tape, making him look like a suicide bomber. We used to call it "hide and go meat".

Pot roast, steaks, pork chops, you name it, we were lucky enough to have it. It seemed like everything they cooked was fried in vegetable oil. To make matters worse, my grandparents would fry eggs and potatoes in bacon grease that sat in a jelly jar on top of the counter. My grandmother made her spaghetti sauce with pork, beef, and veal, and it was probably a 3,000 calorie portion serving.

Her breaded chicken had about 4 inches of breadcrumb, talk about debauchery! You literally had to bite down hard to get to any chicken. Everything was delicious, but unfortunately now I realize they were killing themselves off slowly with their diet or lack thereof. Salt was thrown around by the handful during dinner, as the salt shaker was more of an unused novelty item that sat on the table for amateurs.

My grandparents' generation lacked the information we now have about diet and exercise to lessen the risk of heart attack and stroke. But even if they did have it, I honestly don't think they would have changed their diets one bit. It was so culturally ingrained in them, they couldn't imagine eating any other way, it's what they lived for.

Now my parents on the other hand, were better off and were able to make it to the twenty first century with advances in medical treatments and armed with the knowledge of how to live a healthy lifestyle. But like with anything else, it's what you do with the information and in my mother's case, she blatantly ignored it.

My mother died five years ago from a heart attack, and this one conversation I had with her a year before she died still haunts me to this day.

I was visiting her one day and happened to see her blood work results from a recent physical sitting on the kitchen table. Mom was a secret squirrel about her health so for me to find her test results was like hitting the mother load.

Anytime I would ask her how she was feeling, she would always give the standard "Fine" answer, so there was no real gauge to how she was really doing health-wise. Being the nosy detective that I am, I picked up her test results and started reading them. I almost had a heart attack myself when I saw her HDL cholesterol was 365.

"Mom, your cholesterol is too high, you have to eat better" I lectured. Her response was typical. "I like to eat what I like to eat, I don't tell you what to eat anymore so mind your own business".

The numbers didn't lie and were staring her right in the face like a flashing caution light. But she was content to eat whatever she wanted, whenever she wanted to her peril, despite what her doctor and I preached.

Some of you will read this and say I was a shitty son because I could have done more to help my mother. Here I am writing a book about debauchery and death risks and I couldn't help my own mother. Let me say this about her: she was so impenetrable in her beliefs that she could have been an element on the periodic table.

Just reading her test results and challenging her took balls on my part, and could have been grounds for dismissal in her eyes. If I would have said much more about her cholesterol, she would have locked me out of the house the next time I showed up for a visit. She didn't want to hear it, end of story.

The generation born in the 1940s, who lived in the five boroughs of New York City were very reluctant to change. They weren't stupid people by any means, but were very stubborn and in my mother's case, stubbornness and reluctance to change were her downfall.

My father tried to eat a little healthier later in life but his diet was less than ideal. When I would question what he was eating he would say, "What do you want, to live forever?" or "Your health food sucks, I would rather enjoy life now pal, than eat that crap and live longer".

I never thought of sushi as health food but my father could not wrap his head around eating raw fish or anything raw for that matter. One time, coming out of a sushi restaurant in my neighborhood, I ran into him and one of his AARP buddies whom I hadn't met before.

"Frank, I would like you to meet my son Vic, he eats raw fish and is very healthy. He is going to live fifteen minutes longer than the rest of us, now get out of here, jerkoff" he said as he waved me off.

I just stood there with my mouth hanging open, looking like an idiot.

What can you say to that? He sawed my legs off and dismissed me in front of his codger pal in one fell swoop. Like I said, that generation from the Bronx was stubborn. They loved their red meat, and nothing was going to stop them from eating it, no matter how much of a pain in the ass I was.

Come to think of it my father did like fish, but the problem was my mother didn't. If he ever asked her to cook fish, she would complain about it all week. Then on game day, she would fry it in a skillet at 600 degrees in olive oil, setting off every smoke detector in the house.

She would complain about the smell and how the skin stuck to the pan. As if to martyrize the skillet, she would let it soak in the sink for 3 days just to remind everyone of the dangers of frying fish. After permeating the house with the smell of burnt fish, she would open all the widows, even if it was January.

Then she would spray Glade fart spray all over the house until we couldn't breathe. I wonder if it ever occurred to her that the smell of burnt fish was much better than the Asian whore house scent she sprayed us with.

My mother would put on this Siegfried & Roy performance every year hoping my father wouldn't have the balls to ask her to cook fish again. Believe me, she knew what she was doing, and yes he had the balls to ask her to cook fish again.

If you think that was bad, you should have seen the dog and pony show she put on when my father requested liver and onions.

Before you see a doctor or pharmacist, don't you think it's a good idea to do some preventative maintenance? Like a well maintained car, what you put into it is what you get out. If you're the guy who buys cheap gas or gets your oil changed every fifteen thousand miles at some low budget pit stop who employs parolees and uses recycled motor oil, you're not going to get 100,000 miles out of your car.

Taking shortcuts with your car is going to hurt performance as well as its lifespan. Eventually your engine will gunk up and seize, or you're going to need a new fuel pump and injectors because of the cheap gasoline you've been using.

Using my car analogy, if you eat right and exercise and don't abuse your body, you should live longer. The problem is some of us choose to run on inferior fuels. Nutrition plays a large role in longevity and staying out of the doctor's office. I'm not advocating becoming a vegan or making your own yogurt, but you cannot eat meat and pasta with every meal and expect to be svelte.

We all like to enjoy ourselves when eating, but any doctor will tell you the key to staying healthy is moderation. The dynamics of the American family and diet for that matter changed years ago when mom went into the workplace leaving dad and the kids to fend for themselves at mealtime.

Today's American family does not have time for a home cooked meal, which was replaced with fast food or processed microwaveable food. It will do in a pinch but to live off that crap day in and day out, you're looking for the diverticulosis.

If you're really looking to go out with a bang, try the NYPD diet. Nobody eats worse than cops, trust me, I know. I worked plenty of midnight shifts in terrible neighborhoods that don't offer sushi or green tea. Inedible pizza or Jamaican beef patties washed down with coffee or soda are on the menu. If you're lucky, you may find a Chinese takeout place that hasn't recently been closed down by the board of health. The chop suey is loaded with enough MSG and sodium, you're lucky you don't vapor lock right after ingesting it.

It's inevitable that we are all going to die at some point because we all have an expiration date, but you don't have to sprint to the finish line to get there. Just because there are cholesterol lowering drugs, doesn't mean you should throw caution to the wind and eat like you're going to the electric chair after enjoying your last meal. Strategically placed cholesterol lowering drug commercials are aired when people are eating at their worst, watching sports on weekends.

It's a party atmosphere with friends and family gathering to enjoy a Sunday of football. Everybody brings a different dish laden with meat and cheese and the fridge is packed with ice cold beer. What better way to justify eating badly than doing it with a bunch of enablers, I mean, friends.

During a commercial break, you look up at the TV and see a fat guy wearing an orange Winnie the Pooh fleece and friar Tuck bald spot. Friar Tuck has just been told his cholesterol is 600, obviously upsetting news. He shouldn't worry though because this new wonder drug is going to enable him to eat like he's perpetually on a cruise ship.

The moron begins to celebrate like he won the grand prize on "The Price Is Right". A fake doctor appears explaining he's a fake doctor while Friar Tuck moonwalks with a slice of pizza hanging out of his mouth. As Friar Tuck tries to induce a heart attack before taking his first pill, the fake doctor reads off the list of side effects.

Not once does the fake doctor mention the new stent they snaked through the friar's balls or possible anal leakage. Never do they show Friar Tuck's wife crying in a corner because the new wonder drug is going to put a damper on the spending spree the life insurance policy would have paid when the good friar croaked.

You don't have to look too far for examples of obese people begging for a heart attack or stroke. How many times do you have to visit Disney World to witness some Henry VIII looking guy with a turkey leg hanging out of his mouth? Or the pear shaped woman sporting cankles at the condiment station, pumping cheese with 2 hands on her nachos grande next to her 64 ounce soda.

Go to any theme park in Orlando and watch grossly overweight geriatrics ride motorized scooters, laboring to pull their massive weight. Watch as they bark commands at their walking relatives in the brutal Florida sun, ordering them to pass the King sized Snickers.

I recently visited Germany and they like to eat and drink over there too, but there's a big difference. They may be big boned but they are in shape. Germans are always walking, biking, or doing some form of physical activity. I didn't see too many muffin tops or protruding stomachs when I was there.

You have lots of choices when it comes to exercise. You can walk, run, bike, or join a gym. You can exercise alone or do it with a friend.

Exercise is a double edged sword and can be really good for your health, if you don't overdo it. Over exercise and you can seriously injure yourself. We live in a vain society and everyone wants to look good.

Next time you're in the doctor's office, take a look at the magazines they leave out. It's all slim, tan models with blinding white smiles, wearing the latest fashions. Those magazines really don't reflect society, although most of us secretly strive to look that way. If you don't work out or watch what you eat after age 30, chances are you're going to look like shit.

Join one of those dungeon-like crossfit gyms in an industrial park without supervision and you could wind up falling off a 50 foot rope onto a concrete floor. So what do you do?

You have three roads, so choose wisely my son. You can watch what you eat, exercise, and live a healthy lifestyle. You can be a couch potato, eat too much and suffer death by platano. Or you can join a gym, out of shape, without proper training or equipment, over exert yourself and suffer death by stupidity.

Medical science has shown exercise aids in longevity. Doctors recommend some form of exercise to lower blood pressure, cholesterol, and aid in avoiding a whole host of ailments. So maybe you should give some thought to joining a local gym.

January 1st Syndrome

I am all for setting goals if they are realistic, not pie in the sky pipedreams. Why is it that people think the best time to get into shape is right after New Year's Eve? Did they forget about the other 364 days of the year?

The gym sounds like a safe place to get in shape, right? There are free weights, machines, and a pool, all with personal trainers to whip you into shape. What could go wrong?

Let's start with that New Year's resolution you made to finally get in shape. Your neighborhood gym is huge and from the outside, you can see all the hot chicks working out behind floor to ceiling windows. Over the weekend, you decide to stop in to kick the tires and take a tour of the gym.

You're met at the front desk by a meathead sporting a buzz cut, who couldn't quite cut it as a used car salesman. In his mind, small as it is, he's got the best of both worlds. He can work out all day long, pick up hot chicks and sell gym memberships. Most of his paycheck goes to the GNC vitamin store located in the same plaza, where he buys questionable supplements and protein bars. His bronze tan reminds you of a dirty penny. He's wearing a polo shirt two sizes too small, making his arms look huge. This is not a man who uses the low tumble dry setting on his dryer.

Meathead tells you the gym offers a free evaluation session with a personal trainer to assess your overall fitness level. In reality it's the trainer's job to beat your ass and make you feel like shit. The idea being after your ass kicking, you'll want to buy a gym membership because you're worthless and weak and tired of getting sand kicked in your face. As a motivational tool, the walls are lined with photos of shirtless men sporting man boobs to make you feel better.

While Meathead is grabbing a power bar, you see other meatheads leading postmenopausal women in 1980s Jane Fonda workout ensembles around the gym. Bright colored spandex bottoms show off a variety of different size camel toes. These women have forgotten the cardinal rule, "spandex is a privilege, not a right".

Looking around some more, you observe all sorts of bizarre activity. Another personal trainer ignores an older woman on a treadmill going 60 mph while he texts his steroid connection.

In another corner, a meathead throws a 45 pound medicine ball at a 70 year old geriatric wearing black dress socks. High calf socks and Bruce Jenner headbands litter the gym like dandelions in a field. It looks like the color blind have raided the clearance rack at the Salvation Army.

Meathead looks at you with disgust and asks, "What are your workout goals, bro?"

You explain that it's been a while since you've been in the gym and just want to lose a few pounds and stay in shape. "No problem bro", he says, leading you around the gym like a lackey, while drinking from a one gallon jug of water he's lugging around. "Gotta hydrate bro", he lectures.

As your guide takes you on your safari around the gym, you run into a cast of characters that doubles as professional wrestlers. Built like steroid action figures, they too carry around the one gallon jugs and dutifully line up at the fountain. As you watch this phenomenon, you are reminded of Sally Struthers in a Care commercial, begging you for money to help an African village obtain water.

In the back of the gym, the juice bar has antifreeze colored drinks for five dollars a pop. A guy dressed like Dog The Bounty Hunter with the IQ of a bottle rocket, operates a blender, making foul smelling smoothies, never once bothering to wash the blender pitcher in between drinks.

If you thought the old people dressed bizarre at the gym, the so called workout warriors have their own clothing line. Young Turks pump iron while admiring themselves in the mirror, wearing Timberland boots and hooded sweatshirts with knit wool caps pulled over their heads.

They seem to make a lot of unnecessary noise, screaming at the top of their lungs as if they ruptured a testicle. Lady Gaga blasts from speakers high above, while metal weights slam to the ground. A bowling alley seems quiet in comparison to this place.

You look into the pool, well you really shouldn't have looked into the pool, and you're lucky you didn't turn to stone from what you just witnessed. Geriatric women wearing Esther Williams shower caps, quasi swim at a snail's pace in their swimming lanes. They stop about five times per lap to stand up and stretch their varicose veins.

The pool guy must have been a WWII Nazi scientist because a chlorine gas fog hovers over the water. With forty urinary tract infections last month, Klaus is going heavy on the chlorine.

All the while, Meathead is running you around like a hamster on a wheel, making you use every exercise machine the gym has to offer while he admires his tribal tattoo in every mirror he passes.

You inquire about workout classes and Meathead explains that "Juggernaut" and "Armageddon" are their advanced Pilates classes, although "Tiptoe Zumba" is better suited for pussies like you.

In the background you hear 1970s porno music coming from the Yoga class, where you see uncoordinated geriatrics stretching on the floor. It looks interesting enough though and you wonder if you would ever have the balls to try it.

You give Meathead the slip and duck into a spin class that's in session. The instructor is in Pippi Longstocking pigtails, and is screaming at her class to peddle faster and faster like an Alaskan musher. Eva Braun notices you have entered her class and gives you a scowl like you shit in her Easter basket for coming in late.

Eva has the heat turned up to a balmy 85 degrees and you notice a couple of people dropping off their cycles like they just completed the Bataan Death March. You decide this is not for you and turn to leave, but not before Eva calls you a bitch and tells you to shut the door behind you.

To try something more your pace, you jump on the nearest treadmill and slowly start walking. You glance up and notice a small woman with a mustache walking around the gym, carrying a spray bottle and a dirty rag.

You watch as she stops at every third machine, whether it's occupied or not, and sprays the machine and/or person with an odorless clear substance. When she nears your treadmill, you ask her what kind of disinfectant she's using and she answers "yes" with a confused look on her face. It dawns on you that she doesn't speak English but you're now concerned about the cleanliness of the gym, so you ask Meathead about MRSA. He explains they don't carry that protein drink but he can special order it for you.

After your workout, Meathead instructs you like a prison guard to hit the showers and see him on your way out. He has saved the best for last, the locker room. You walk in and cannot help but notice how bright it is in there. All you see are old naked men walk out of blinding light like the "Close encounters of a

3rd kind". Can't they dim the lights in here to camouflage all the sagging testicles?

You notice the yellow plastic sign cautioning you to the wet floor. It's too late though; you've already committed and stepped on a Bouncing Betty. With no place to go, you find yourself standing in 2 inches of water, pouring out of a urinal like Niagara Falls, soaking your Reeboks.

Naked fat men wandering around with their balls dragging a few inches off the floor is not what you wanted to see on your day off. Towels seem to be optional here, forcing you to make eye contact with everyone as you don't want to be accused of being a "pecker checker".

After taking a shower, old men practice a macabre ritual of drying their wet testicles using the wall dryer. As they lean their chestnuts into the hot air, the smell of burnt pubic hair permeates the locker room. When they're done, they stand in front of a large wall mirror trimming their pubes with a pair of scissors, sending ball hair cascading to the floor. The old timers treat the locker room like it's their own bathroom, planting their ancient asses on any flat surface.

Against better judgement, you muster up the courage to use the toilet. All the urinals are in use and it looks like a geriatric pissing firing squad. Enlarged prostates make codgers crowd the plate like Barry Bonds, forcing their crotches into the porcelain. Weak piss streams splash the rock candy below resulting in yet another unpleasant odor.

You enter the toilet stall and close the door behind you. You slowly turn around and realize you're fucked. You are greeted by a foot long anaconda turd and you get the sense that braver men than you have tried to flush it away before.

The toilet seat has more DNA on it than a crime scene, and no amount of toilet paper you put between your ass and the seat is going to save you.

You make it out of the locker room by the skin of your balls and decide you have had enough of this circus for the day. You make an attempt to avoid Meathead at Checkpoint Charlie, but he snags you at the front door. Meathead gives it one last ditch effort to close the deal.

"How many years you going to sign up for bro?" he asks. Your head's spinning and you just want to get the hell out of there. You tell him you want to mull it over a few days, thank him for his time and make your escape.

By the time you get home, Meathead has left 3 messages on your answering machine, lowering the price of membership with each call. He also mentions they are running a special on MRSA this week if you join the gym today.

If you find a gym you're comfortable with and can afford, by all means join. If you want to buy a workout DVD and leave skid marks on your rug like a dog, you can do that too.

Listen to your doctor, put down the HO-HO, and walk to the store instead of driving 2 blocks. Instead of opening the back door and letting your dog decorate the backyard with hot steamers, take him out for a walk and get a little exercise. Join the rest of the world picking up fresh dog shit with a plastic bag which you had to beg for at your local supermarket. Carry it around for the remainder of your walk, while waving to your idiot suburban neighbors who insist on stopping you and letting their dog sniff your dog's ass.

Try to force a smile while they hold you hostage, forcing you to listen to their mindless bullshit. To increase cardio during your crap walk, swing your bag of dog shit high over your head like hunting bolas. Think of yourself as a gaucho on the hunt warding off tedious conversations with moronic neighbors. I promise you, you'll be the topic of conversation at the next homeowners' association meeting.

Since you're reading this book, chances are you don't go to those meetings anyway, nor do you give a fuck what people say about you.

Now if you come from a family of athletes and decathlon winners with no history of heart disease, good for you, that's wonderful, just keep reading anyway.

You don't have to kill yourself with exercise but doing something is a lot better than doing nothing. It's like anything thing else worthwhile in life, what you put in is usually what you will get out.

Taking shortcuts will not ensure the same results. Taking a pill to lose weight or lower your cholesterol is a shortcut. You could just as easily watch what you eat or perform some type of exercise. So get out there and keep that heart pumping!

Chapter 4

Trust Your Doctor But Ask Questions Anyway

You can't put a price on your life, can you? Unfortunately a lot of us do and would rather spend our money on something frivolous rather than pay for better medical care. Most of us are going to die from some disease or medical ailment. Some will be a result of heredity, stupidity, or just plain bad luck. Did you ever stop to think who and where you sought medical attention from may play a role in your longevity?

Unfortunately many die every year from not asking medical professionals questions about procedures, medications, or the medical facilities they are being treated in. Oftentimes we trust medical professionals blindly and follow their orders like sheep herded into a pen.

We live in a time where medical advances seem to leapfrog one another. They say if you can live the next ten years, you will see the next fifty. Hopefully that's true but what's confusing is what we thought was good for us not too long ago, is bad for us today. Google any disease, treatment, supplement, or vegetable for that matter and see what you get. A hodgepodge of study after study contradicting one another.

Medical science mimics a Tom Harris spy novel with spooks trading sides constantly spreading misinformation. Eat grapefruit, don't eat grapefruit, eat meat, don't eat meat - the contradicting reports are maddening.

I'm 50 years old and I remember the 1970s like if it was yesterday. Red meat was good for you and disco was hot. Women smoked during their pregnancies and fire retardant children's pajamas were the rave. Now beef is not always for dinner, getting replaced by the more expensive fish. Children now press their faces against the microwave oven while nuking a hot pocket and mom shoves a tube in a different hole to take her kid's temperature.

Yeah the 70s was a cutting edge time, wasn't it? How bad could vegetable oil be? It comes from vegetables, right? We had ear wax colored margarine over butter and soda at the dinner table. The soybean was a miracle bean that was going to solve world hunger and we were all going to convert to the metric system while singing Kumbaya.

What a load of bullshit. If you're in your 70s and reading this you're probably calling those of us who hail from Generation X a bunch of pussies, and rightfully so. How can you compare living through polio, measles, and black and white television to my generation's problems?

My gastroenterologist was explaining the preparation I would have to endure for my dreaded colonoscopy. I was scared shitless so to speak, and really didn't want to go through the procedure but I was pushing 50 so I figured I had better man up and get "the pipe". I had never had any form of invasive medical procedure before so this was all new to me.

The snake charmer explained there were several laxatives I could take to clean myself out the night before.

"Which medication is the best?" I asked

"Well the better laxative works faster and usually won't give you any stomach cramps" he explained.

"That's the one I want" I said.

"Are you sure, that's the most expensive one and your insurance may not cover it" my doctor replied. I couldn't care less what it cost.

"If that's the best medication write me a script and I will pick it up", I replied.

"You know, most people go the other way and purchase the less expensive laxative" my doctor said.

"Why would they do that if it would lessen their discomfort?"

"When it comes to medicine, people will always ask 'how much' and opt for the least expensive option" he said. "People tell me all the time I don't get paid enough for being a doctor". But once I mention what it's going to cost, they don't want to pay for it" he said. "If they were buying a flat screen TV or jet ski, they wouldn't ask about price. But when it comes to their health they will only go for as much as their insurance covers" he explained.

I walked out of his office scratching my head. How much more could a superior laxative be? Ten, twenty, thirty bucks? I knew the upcoming procedure was going to be a pain in the ass so to speak. I just wanted to get it over with as easy as possible. One way or the other, I knew I would be up all night with a bottle of Yoo Hoo rocketing out of my ass at 300 psi. Why wouldn't I try to make it as painless as possible, avoiding the cramps that come along with the procedure?

Most of us are afraid to ask our medical professionals simple questions. Choosing the right doctor or hospital can save your life. If you got fucked over by an auto mechanic who never really fixed your car, overcharged you, and showed no interest in you, would you go back? You would tell that mechanic to go fuck himself and you'd find another one.

People go back to the same doctors though because they tend to trust someone who they perceive knows more than they do, or who wears a white coat (or costume). Those who wear surgical scrubs, black robes, or mouse ears should all be taken seriously.

After I got my nose broken playing softball, I found an ear nose and throat guy who accepted my insurance plan. A neighbor of mine is a nurse and she asked me who I was going to see. When I told her, she replied "Oh, he's kinda old and not the best, you should see someone else".

I blew off her advice and went to my appointment. His office was in an old building in a shitty part of town. The office manager slid open an opaque glass partition to greet me. She looked so much like Mr. Rooney's secretary in "Ferris Bueller's Day Off", I almost called her Grace. After I filled out the questionnaire, she went into the attorney's office next door to photocopy my insurance card.

"We share a copy machine", she explained.

As I sat in that outdated 1970s office that smelled of mold, I realized the joke was on me. Bored, I started looking at his college degrees mounted on the Brady bunch wood paneling. 1969??

"This guy graduated medical school in 1969" I said to myself. "Lyndon B Johnson was president, I was three years old drinking Tang and Neil Armstrong was playing golf on the moon. A lot has changed since then. How fucking old is this guy?"

I started getting nervous, thinking maybe my neighbor was right and I should see someone else. Fight or flight was kicking in and I was just about to get up and run out when the door opened.

He greeted me wearing a metal halo contraption strapped to his forehead like an old-timey TV doctor. "I have to get the fuck out of here" I said to myself. All I could think of was that this guy was going to shove a tuning fork up my nose and do a rhinoplasty adjustment right here in his office.

I decided to let him see me anyway and after examining me, he told me my nose didn't need a fine tuning. Needless to say I was relieved. No news is good news and I ran out of his office.

"What if this had been for my heart or liver" I said to myself. I'm never going to see a clown like this again no matter what the cost.

Another time I had a mole on my arm and I figured I would get it checked out. I flipped through my health care provider's booklet where I found a dermatologist 2.5 miles away from my house. "How great is this, he's around the corner" I said to myself.

I arrived at his office and went to the front desk to sign in. On the receptionist's desk were CDs for sale and on the cover was a guy in a tuxedo and cowboy hat holding a guitar. "This is kind of odd" I said to myself. I asked the receptionist, "Who is that?"

"That's Dr. Smith, his country music CDs are available for sale!"

This fucking clown is supplementing his medical practice by selling his country music out of his office? I tore up the questionnaire as I walked back through the parking lot, and no, I did not buy his CD.

What good is the flat screen or new car if you're dead? Do you want a new toy or do you want to be alive? If you have insurance coverage like mine, there is a list of providers you can choose from. I personally like doctors from the northeast. I'm not in the business of recommending doctors but if I cannot pronounce your name or never heard of your college, I'm not going to see you.

Death by Embarrassment

Just because a doctor writes you a prescription doesn't mean you shouldn't ask questions about the medication or an alternative method. He's an educated man, not God almighty, so it's ok to question him. Fuck him if he doesn't like it, it's your body and your copayment. It seems that over the last twenty years, doctors have been over prescribing medications.

If you don't believe me, why have antibiotic resistant bacteria and a lot of zombies hooked on oxycodone popped up over the last couple of years? Society has decided it needs a prescription after leaving the doctor's office and the doctors are more than willing to throw pills at you to shut you up. If a condition can be resolved by diet or lifestyle change, why are you taking a pill?

I am not anti-drug or into holistic medicine, but doctors have been prescribing methadone for years and those folks don't seem to be getting any better. Have you ever seen a Methadonian? They aren't the picture of health.

If you're lucky, well you wouldn't be necessarily lucky if you were sitting in a doctor's office waiting room, but the next time you are, watch what happens when the pharmaceutical representative stops in. She's going to be very attractive and dressed to kill. In one arm she's got a briefcase containing samples of the new wonder drug from Devlin MacGregor, and lunch for the office staff in the other. My mother warned me about strangers offering candy, and she was right.

The doctor is usually pretty busy so if he's not trying to bang her, he has his caporegime office manager deal with her. The doctor cannot accept kickbacks from a pharmaceutical company for prescribing their drugs because that would be unethical. But like in the movie "The Fugitive", they can take doctors on all expense paid vacations, I mean seminars, at exclusive resorts.

Give that some thought the next time you have a 30 second consultation with your doctor after which he writes you a prescription for a new drug that sounds like an undiscovered solar system.

Let's say you *are* happy with your doctor's diagnosis and he writes you a prescription. You're not out of the woods yet, here comes the tricky part. You have to head over to your pharmacy to get the prescription filled. Your pharmacist will then hand you your medication along with a fifteen page instructional booklet explaining all the reasons why you really shouldn't be taking this drug. As he hands you your prescription, he will ask "Do you have any questions?"

You are now at a proverbial fork in the road. If you're taking multiple medications or you're familiar with this drug from a TV commercial asking you to call an 800 number for a pending class action lawsuit, stop and think.

Are you going to be the guy who takes five minutes and says "Yes, I do have a question" to the nice man in the white coat who looks like he should be selling ice cream? Or are you going to roll the dice with your life and stay silent? Do you risk the scorn of angry cotton tops behind you in line that have no other place to go besides the incontinence aisle? Or do you leave, pills in hand without answers?

Screw the dirty looks and mumbling behind you and ask your question. It could be the last question you never asked.

Choosing the right hospital can also save your life. If you're hearing stories about patients getting antibiotic resistant bacteria or surgeons operating on the wrong lung at the hospital you're about to visit for a procedure, stop and think. Consult your doctor, the board of health, or ask Siri for Christ sake, just take charge of your life and ask questions.

Living in Denial

I knew a guy who had just entered the early stages of diabetes. His doctor told him that since they caught the disease early enough, he could avoid insulin pills if he changed his diet. One would think that after getting this news, a lifestyle change would be in order, right?

Wrong. I never met a guy who wanted to lose his toes so badly, besides sandals aren't in style anyway. I would watch in amazement as he would eat license plate size Hershey bars and wash them down with a twenty ounce diet soda. He ate bread with every meal and visited the candy machine so often, the joke was he didn't need change because he had a chip implanted in his body so that the machine could scan him for faster service.

One day I watched him down 4 twenty ounce diet cokes in an eight hour workday. I tried to explain to him that drinking diet soda tricks your body into producing insulin, and that affects your weight and can cause diabetes. He looked at me like I had three heads.

"Well if losing fingers and going blind don't scare you, how about pissing razor blades because you're going to get kidney stones?" I asked.

He told me to go fuck myself as he had another sip of diet soda. You really can't save someone from themselves.

There is no better investment you can make than in yourself. Spend your money on things that will prolong your life. If people researched hospitals and healthcare professionals like they did a new car, the odds are they would live longer. How long is a new car going to last you, maybe ten years? I think we all want to get more than ten years out of our bodies and getting a competent doctor will increase those odds. The bottom line is doctors are human beings who can be wrong and make mistakes. Don't be afraid to ask questions or get a second opinion. It's your body and your life!

Chapter 5

Dickhead Drivers

Driving is a privilege, not a right. Paraphrased from the New York State Department of Motor Vehicles' Rules and Regulations.

Most of us take for granted that operating a motor vehicle is a privilege, not a right, and that privilege can get you killed. Every day, millions of dickheads get behind the wheel of automobiles putting our lives in danger. When you're a dickhead who doesn't know how to drive, you significantly raise the odds of causing a traffic accident.

Over 30,000 Americans are killed every year in car crashes, about the attendance of a weekend baseball game. Those numbers are significantly lower than they were in the 1970s when cars were unsafe death traps. Back then it was more like 50,000 annual deaths, so we've come a long way with advances in vehicle technology and safety. The drivers on the other hand…

When Henry Ford perfected and manufactured the automobile, never in his wildest dreams could he have envisioned how the world would look today as a result of his innovation. Back in Mr. Ford's day, the automobile was looked upon as a revolutionary toy meant only for those with the means to acquire one. Those lucky enough to purchase an automobile drove on dirt roads through piles of horseshit left behind by somebody else's horse. It was a simpler time with less traffic and fewer assholes on the road. Today's world runs on automobiles and a lot more assholes. Just ask Brooks Hatlen who found out the hard way after his release from Shawshank penitentiary.

If you're over eighteen years old and live in the United States, you probably have a valid driver's license and access to a motor vehicle. There are always some exceptions to the rule though. If you're Amish, you ride a horse drawn buggy and enjoy the smell of horseshit. If you're an anti-conformist hipster living in a large city, you ride the subway and enjoy the smell of piss.

When you operate a motor vehicle, you are in control of your own destiny so to speak. You can go everywhere and anywhere, change direction or choose to sit idle. Seatbelts, airbags, and other innovations have made traveling by motor vehicle a lot safer since Mr. Ford's model T first rolled off the assembly line. With all of these modifications one would think traveling by automobile is pretty safe, right?

Just think back to the good old 1970s when it was footloose and fancy free. It was completely common to see a green country squire station wagon fly by with the back seat down and four kids on their hands and knees playing in the rear area of the car. Never once did parents give a second thought to the possibility of dad having to suddenly slam on the brakes, and the children becoming airborne missiles. What's a couple of concussions if you can keep the kids occupied for that long drive to grandma's? This was long before a morally conscious dinosaur raised your children through a propaganda DVD playing in the back seat of your car.

Thinking back to that time reminds me of how much danger I was in as a child. We had a Datsun b210 that weighed as much as a Pepsi can and would shake every time a truck passed us by.

We also had the bean shaped Ford Pinto that would supposedly turn into a firework if rear ended.

Motor vehicle manufacturers have made today's autos safer through better designs. The one thing Detroit and Japan cannot change is the drivers. If you're a moron or live your life irresponsibly, chances are it's going to reflect in the way you drive. Some drivers lack superior hand eye coordination, while others are self-absorbed assholes who are oblivious to their surroundings. Poor drivers are everywhere and it's not linked to age, gender, or social status.

The reality is every time you get into a vehicle you are taking a risk. You're putting yourself in play with a bunch of strangers who are operating a variety of heavy machines right alongside you, each with different skill and mindsets.

The Young and the Restless

Ah, to be young and free again, without any common sense or responsibility. If you came from another planet and knew nothing about young people, you would think someone in excellent health and in the prime of their lives with catlike reflexes would be the safest of drivers.

Tell that to the insurance companies who pay out millions of dollars in claims every year for youngins who wreck their parents' cars. Once your teenager gets their driver's license, your insurance company is notified through the Department of Motor Vehicles, and they promptly raise your insurance premium significantly.

There are no secrets anymore and it would be easier to hide Whitey Bulger from the FBI than your kid's driver's license from State Farm.

Would you trust somebody with no common sense, emotionally unstable and covered in pimples to operate a three thousand pound piece of heavy machinery? You do if you have a teenager and at some point you're going to have let go and begin the process of letting your teenager drive. Depending on your financial situation or intelligence level, parents have two options in purchasing a car for their all-knowing, impatient adolescent.

Shitbox, Noun

A ratty, poorly maintained motor vehicle over ten years old. Usually found through a Craigslist ad from a total stranger. A shitbox seller will swear on a stack of bibles that his vehicle is in tip top shape. Farting smoke all the way home, it mimics a frightened puppy leaking a variety of fluids on your driveway within minutes. A shitbox will often exceed the purchase price in repairs within six months of purchase.

Safety and aesthetics are often ignored attempting to end your teen's nonstop begging for a car. Working a fulltime job, you don't have the time or energy to spend weekend after weekend shopping for your kid's car. Exhausted from looking and from your teen's nonstop whining, you throw common sense to the wind and purchase them a clunker. You ignore the rust, flaking dandruff paint chips, and duct tape holding the windshield in place. At this point you would give your teenager angel dust to get them to shut the fuck up. You may have silenced your kid for now but your nightmare is far from over.

My motto is, "If the exterior looks like shit, can you imagine what's going on under the hood?" Purchasing a shitbox usually results in the late night "Daddy the car broke down, please come get me" phone call. Purchasing the AAA gold towing package is highly recommended when obtaining a shitbox.

I understand not everyone can afford a new car, so you do what you can to get around. But if you're driving a poorly maintained vehicle older than ten years, you're significantly increasing the odds of getting into a fatal accident.

If you're over forty and continue to drive a shitbox, you're probably of low moral character, living like a roach and can most often be found at a dog track or dive bar.

Now if you're a dickhead suburban parent with money to burn, you can go another route.

Dadalac, Noun

A brand new, high performance automobile purchased for a spoiled suburban teenager. Equipped with enough bells and whistles, it practically guarantees overwhelming a new driver. Dadalacs are sometimes delivered to the dickhead parents' driveway sporting a giant red bow on the roof, thus ensuring everyone in the subdivision notices it.

Purchasing a Dadalac for your teenager will get you mixed reviews. Your kid and their friends will think you're the coolest parent ever. Their parents on the other hand, will think you're a total douche bag for putting them on the spot with their own teenager, who will now demand a brand new car.

Threatening to take the car away from your teen if you catch them driving recklessly is a useless deterrent. Your teenager will lie through their Invisalign teeth, promising you that they are driving safely. I absolutely guarantee you if you had a hidden camera in your kid's car, you would see things differently. Speeding, texting, and trying to impress their friends would make you shit twice and bark at the moon. The car would be back at the dealership or junkyard and junior would be driving a razor scooter if you had any idea how reckless your wonderful teenager was behind the wheel.

Silver Alert

Elderly dickheads present a different risk to society. How can old people drive so slowly yet be so deadly? One would think the older you are, the wiser you become. Well that certainly does not apply to driving. There's no shortage of elderly drivers these days because people are living longer and are reluctant to give up their driving privileges. Driving at a snail's pace, they clog our roads like cholesterol, frustrating the hell out of anyone who wants to drive over 20 miles an hour.

Geriatrics are survivors, "How do you think I made it this far?" they'll say, and they like to surround themselves with as much metal as possible to survive a potential crash. The rest of us can go straight to hell. Lincolns, Cadillacs, the bigger the better, the elderly love piloting long gunships. A Lincoln with a handicap placard is a catastrophe waiting to happen. They'll cross two lanes at a time without signaling in search of a Walgreens incontinence aisle.

It's as if someone dropped them off in another universe to fend for themselves. Ignoring traffic lanes, they glide through parking lots like great white sharks waiting to strike. If you're in an area populated by geriatric drivers, I strongly suggest the five second rule. Better to wait five seconds at a green light than to get T boned by grandma blowing through the intersection while she tells her grandkids stories about how she survived the dust bowl.

A cotton top rattler usually has poor vision and wears blue blocker sunglasses resembling the ones used for arc welding. Daylight is now overrated for Hazel ever since the optometrist hinted she maybe be a candidate for cataracts. The tennis ball that sits atop the radio antenna is a warning sign, equivalent to a rattlesnake's rattle; you should stay away from the silver missile.

Some senior citizens plan their whole lives to retire financially secure, only to throw caution to the wind and end up buying a colossal two hundred foot long RV. If you have the balls to pass one of these things on the highway, you'll notice some old geezer sitting twenty feet in the air looking as helpless as the captain of the Titanic. If that's not bad enough, sometimes these RVs are towing the family car behind, adding yet another sixty feet.

Needless to say, this makes changing lanes safely an impossibility. These behemoth earth movers can easily run you right off the road and be none the wiser. Roaring down America's highways in search of a Cracker Barrel, they cut off and sideswipe unsuspecting drivers with extreme prejudice.

When trailer manufacturers transport a double wide trailer comparable in size, it is required for them to display a sign that reads "Wide Load". If someone over the age of 70 is driving one of these long ass RVs, they too should be required to post a sign that reads "Old fool with too much money".

It's not going to happen because if there is one thing that you can be sure of is that the elderly vote. They live for Election Day and you can be sure they will be at the polls early. You can't get a law passed that will improve overall public safety if it impacts the elderly negatively.

Did you know in most cases you do not need a special driver's license to drive an RV? Did you also know there are only a couple of states that require a road test for driver's license renewal after the age of 75? You think maybe you should pass a physical after 75 to drive a car? When Floyd croaks behind the wheel driving to Walmart, his Cadillac has now become a suburban cruise missile.

It's gotten so bad in Florida with senior drivers and dementia, when one goes off the reservation with their car the state issues what's called a silver alert. Television news and digital billboards flash images of the missing codger and their license plate number.

I think it's a lot safer to test a driver over 80 years old for cognitive recognition than to force the public to play "Where's Waldo" when a 90 year old wanders off in her Cadillac looking for her mother. You pray someone notices her church dress blowing from beneath her car door, flying like a flag before they get themselves killed.

The AARP, gray panthers, and blue haired mafia all vote in blocks and would never allow a law requiring retesting or physical standards for operating a motor vehicle. The day a politician proposes a law impacting the elderly negatively is the end of that politician's career.

If there's any upside to elderly drivers, it's that they can only kill you between the hours of 7am to 5pm, so plan your day accordingly.

Not Your Mama's Minivan

Yes, mamas can be dickheads too and nothing personifies this more than the family minivan. If you thought we had too many media distractions in the home, we now have them in our vehicles as well, to aid in keeping our eyes off the road. I thought having an AM/FM radio and cassette player in my first car was pretty cool. Now we have CD and DVD players, XM radio, iPod and God knows what else. Shouldn't driving be just driving? Who came up with the notion that we need to be entertained while driving a motor vehicle?

Drive by any elementary or middle school in the morning and you'll see narcissistic, yoga pant wearing soccer moms hauling ass out of the parking lot en route to the gym. Sporting Ray

Bans, they resemble Top Gun fighter pilots with ponytails held together by industrial strength scrunchies.

With only six hours of freedom, they maintain a ridiculous schedule trying to do fifteen things at once. Speeding through school safety zones they themselves lobbied for at the last PTA meeting, they are oblivious to their surroundings. They drive with their heads down because they're texting their spin class instructor to say they'll be thirty seconds late for class, all the while sipping a one thousand calorie skinny mocha latte.

Spin class? My mother didn't have time for spin class. After we left for school in the morning, my mother cleaned the house and made sure dinner was ready for that evening, two lost arts now gone by the wayside. My mother didn't drive so we walked, and later took public transportation to school. She and her friends didn't double park in front of our school clogging traffic for miles to pick us up. My brother Fredo and I figured it out and made it back home alive. Imagine that, kids actually walking home from school. Today's mother takes extraordinary precautions to protect herself and her precious cargo; her children.

Minivans these days resemble an armored personnel carrier with shiny rims and tinted glass. Mom spared no expense picking out this baby. The Hercules model also comes equipped with the self-involved package and vanity plates. Options include a rear mounted DVD player so that your children can watch a self-righteous singing dinosaur teaching moral lessons while you drive.

With the press of a button, mom can activate dual sliding side doors that allow the children to spill out into the school parking lot while the van is still in motion. This saves mom precious time and exercise energy since she doesn't have to get out of the van to say goodbye. But the distractions don't end there. The new mommy van also comes equipped with Yoga mat racks and "Bitch in the Box" GPS system.

It's no secret that the stay-at-home moms and non-moms who drive minivans have to enlighten the world of how wonderful and complete their families are. White stencil stick figures etched onto the rear window of her minivan indicate how many kids and pets are in the family.

If you're still not getting the hint of how wonderful her family is, here's another clue. The rear bumper of her minivan is littered with bumper stickers telling the world her child is an honor student in middle school, like everyone else's kid.

Texting messages the length of the Magna Carta at a stop light can be tricky. When the light changes, mom continues to argue with spell check that "ceviche" is in fact an actual word. With horns blaring from angry motorists behind her, mom slams on the gas without looking. "Whoomp, there it is". The internationally known sound of metal hitting metal is heard. Some poor bastard who thought cool mom was giving him the right of way makes a turn in front of her, only to get blasted through no fault of his own.

No matter how you slice it, a minivan is a minivan. Despite how many bells and whistles it has, it's a mailbox, plain and simple. It's a box to transport your children around and not a coolmobile. I'm guessing children are distracting enough that you don't need any more stimulation inside the cabin of your minivan.

Aftermarket Morons

For the most part, auto manufacturers know what they are doing while building a car. Every now and then they inadvertently make a mistake or have a defect resulting in deaths or injuries which they deny or ignore, resulting in class action lawsuits, but I digress.

Auto manufactures are regulated by our government and spend billions on vehicle safety. When you drive a new car off the lot, for the most part, you're getting a safe vehicle. It's brand spanking new and baptized by the manufacturer with a guaranteed warranty for several years. It's perfect, so why do people take it upon themselves to modify their vehicles?

We've all seen some jackass or half assed mechanic alter their car or truck for no apparent reason other than to look like a mamaluke. I thought the Bronx was bad with that shit. When I moved to Florida, I couldn't believe the sheer amount of hillbillies who modify their cars and trucks to look badass. I thought all that crap ended when the Dukes of Hazzard went off the air!

If you're converting your pickup truck into a bunk bed with monster truck tires so that a ladder is required to climb into it, you're looking to die sooner rather than later. The higher up you go the easier it is to tip over, it's common sense, isn't it?

I was always under the impression that the better you can see, the better you can drive. Tell that to these schmucks who tint their windows so dark, the interior resembles a lunar eclipse with zero visibility. You think looking out a window that dark at night may impair your vision? You bet your sister's ass it does!

Why would you replace new, manufacturer tested and approved tires and rims with aftermarket wafer thin ones that'll go flat if you hit a pebble?

Like I said earlier, Detroit and Japan know what they are doing. Stop playing mad scientist, pimping out your car or truck and putting your life and the lives of others at risk.

Drinking and Driving

Drinking and driving is a sure fire way to ruin several lives at once. I am not a member of MADD but it's fairly obvious that if you drink and drive something very bad can happen. The possibility of killing yourself or someone else with your car should be enough of a deterrent to call a cab.

If you drink and have a driver's license, chances are you have or will drink and drive. Police departments are federally funded to arrest drunk drivers. They receive the resources for DUI training, vehicles and overtime to conduct roadblocks and specialized units to locate and arrest drunk drivers. When the federal government gets involved with something criminal, it's over. Ask Al Capone, John Gotti or Martha Stewart what happens when you don't play nice with the feds.

If there is one thing I know it's that nobody likes to get pulled over by the police. I was a cop for twenty years myself, and the few times I've gotten pulled over for something, my heart would pound. If you're drinking and driving imagine the feeling you're going to have when you see those flashing lights in your rear view mirror. You know what you did and there's no way out of it. Imagine the horror you're going to experience for the next couple of hours after your arrest.

Say you're lucky and get arrested for DUI without an accident. You're still going to have your driver's license either modified or suspended. You're going to get put on probation and will be assigned an overworked probation officer who will treat you like a scumbag. Once a month, you're going to have to sit around in a room for an hour with real criminals while you wait to see him. After he talks down to you for 10 minutes, he will march you into a bathroom and demand you piss in a cup in front of him. At this point you should be saying to yourself, "I should have just downloaded the Uber app and avoided all this bullshit."

Not So Smart

Before I close this chapter, I feel the need to take a swipe at Smart Cars and their owners. Whose bright idea was it to call something small, slow, and unsafe "Smart"?

I understand advertisement agencies will say anything to sell something, but come on people, you've been duped. It's ignoring the obvious whether you want to accept it or not. Smart Cars remind me of the toy cars we rolled around on the carpet as kids. I'll bet you those toy cars had more horsepower. Nothing that can be totaled by a moped or a fat chick is "Smart". Just imagine how a Smart Car would hold up after getting hit by a truck.

Sometimes I don't have enough time to find a gas station and I let my fuel tank run dangerously low. Can you imagine looking for a power strip or whatever you have to plug that piece of shit into? People who drive Smart Cars are socially conscious and want to save the environment. After you're killed in your micro machine you can save a tree and get buried in your crushed Coke can.

If you want to live longer and not perish in a vehicle accident, you need to take these five necessary steps.

1. Drive a newer or well-maintained vehicle
2. Avoid elderly drivers
3. Don't drink and drive
4. Surround yourself with as much metal as possible
5. Pay attention!

Chapter 6

Murder Is Forever

Murder Is Forever is not the latest James Bond movie. No special effects or hoopla, just good ole fashioned violent death. It's a catchy name for a chapter isn't it? Death sells and if you don't believe me, ask your local funeral home director. You obviously must agree or you wouldn't have spent your money on a book about death.

I never promised you a rose garden when you ponied up $3.99 for the book so grow up. Murder is an interactive way to die, and like in square dancing, you'll need a partner who in this case, is willing to take your life. Man is the only animal that will kill for his own selfish reasons. Most species will only kill for food or protection. When a shark attacks a swimmer it's because it has mistakenly thought the swimmer was a food source. In fairness to the shark, after it realizes its mistake and you're not a sea lion, it's usually on his way to another buffet. Some animals will attack if they perceive you might be getting to close to their young or for self-preservation, but that's about it.

Man has always and will always kill for a whole host of selfish reasons and in some cases, for no reason at all. From cavemen to present day, man has used murder as an absolute way to solve his problems. Some will give into their emotions, putting aside the fact that killing someone will often bring on greater problems. The thought of incarceration, retribution or just good old fashioned guilt is outweighed by instant gratification.

There are institutions all over the world filled with men and women in brightly colored jumpsuits, behind bars as a result of their inability to control their temper and behavior. The bizarre thing about murder is that when someone makes the conscious, or as a defense attorney would argue, unconscious decision to take a life, they have in effect forfeited their own. Nothing will ever be the same again. If you kill someone, you will spend the rest of your life or at least a good portion of it in prison reflecting on your deeds with other scumbags. If you're not caught initially, you will be looking over your shoulder waiting for the day it catches up to you.

Whether or not you are arrested for it, you have committed the ultimate sin. Make all the lazy cop jokes you want, but if you want to get a cop out of a Dunkin Donuts, go kill someone and see what happens. Law enforcement tends to take that sort of thing seriously.

If you're feeling strong and have the balls, go ask the mafia or your local drug gang how seriously. I'm just kidding, I really don't recommend you doing that, it might get you killed. Don't get me wrong, criminals are more than willing to clip someone if they get in the way or challenge their criminal enterprise.

But murder is bad for business, bringing a lot of bad press and heat. Even if the police don't solve a murder right away, but know who is responsible for it, there are serious repercussions and a lot of unwanted attention.

To give you an example, in 1988 a low level mafia associate named Costabile Farace murdered DEA agent Everett Hatcher during the course of an undercover drug buy operation in Staten Island, New York. After the murder, Farace went into hiding in the NYC area. It didn't take long for the NYPD to figure out who Farace and his friends were. The amount of pressure applied to the mafia crippled their finances. During the time Farace was a fugitive, I was at the Whitestone auto pound dropping off a stolen car. In the back lot I saw hundreds of the large, old style satellite dishes you used to see on roofs before Direct TV came around.

"What's with the satellite dishes?" I asked. The cop at the pound informed me that our organized crime units had been hitting all the gambling dens and sports book operations in the city. To break the mafia's balls after the raids, they would tear down the satellite dishes and voucher them as evidence, sending them off to the pound. The mafia makes millions of dollars every year on illegal sports betting and the satellite dishes enable them to run their business effectively. During that time period so much pressure was applied to the mafia families, they figured Mr. Farace was not worth the trouble of hiding. The mob was not about to hand him over to the police for prosecution; they are not that kind hearted.

The mafia decided the best way to handle the Farace case was an out of court settlement in street court. When it was all said and done, Farace and one of his friends were found shot dead on a Brooklyn street as sort of an appeasement to law enforcement. They didn't get their satellite dishes back, but things eventually cooled down for them.

There's no statute of limitations for murder, like the genital herpes, it never goes away. If you commit a robbery and are not arrested or indicted for the crime, after 5 years you're home free. You can tell anyone who will listen about it because you cannot be charged for that robbery due to the statute of limitation. No such luck for a murder charge.

Let's say you're one of these idiots who believes everything you see on Dexter. I have no idea why you would be reading this book, but I digress. Your well planned murder goes off without a hitch and the cops never question you about it, so you figure you're not a suspect and you're in the clear.

You're not off the hook just yet so don't go spiking the ball in the end zone, this is far from over. Even if the case runs cold or unsolved for years, that homicide folder will sit in the detective squad waiting for the next new detective to come in with a fresh pair of eyes and perspective to look at it from a different angle.

Murder is the major leagues of crime so to speak. If you're capable of taking a life, you're capable of anything and law enforcement makes it its highest priority to solve the case in terms of resources and talent. Police departments will always throw their best and brightest detectives into homicide units to get murder cases solved.

More often than not, homicide units are comprised of sharp, seasoned detectives who as we used to say, "speak to God". Don't get me wrong, an idiot detective could wind up in a homicide unit but I wouldn't commit a murder in hopes of getting the one moron to investigate my case. Murder never goes away and it brings more trouble than it's worth.

Some people commit murder and will be riddled with guilt forever. Whether captured or not, they live in a self-imposed purgatory in their own minds, reliving their actions over and over again. The vast majority though are sociopaths who could give a shit about their victims or the victim's family. The ends justify the means and they kill for their own selfish reasons that only they can understand.

There never seems to be a shortage of murder as the six o'clock news reminds us daily. Murder does not discriminate and can happen just as easily in a major city or rural farm country.

There is no dignified way to die, but in my opinion murder is the worst way to go. Yes, the cancer is the most painful for both the victim and family members who watch a monster at work. We watch as the cancer transforms a thriving, healthy individual into a weak frail victim, just waiting for life to come to an end. We feel cheated when a loved one suffers a fatal heart attack or passes away in an accident because there were so many things we wanted to say to them. But if you want to talk about the most unfair way to die, murder is the ultimate swindle.

The victim and family are always the last to know. You have zero control while your adversary plays God with your life. Your death can be planned or just a random act of wanton violence. Working in law enforcement for twenty years, I saw plenty of unfortunate souls whose lives were violently cut short at the hands of someone else.

The reasons vary and 99 percent of the time, murder is unjustifiable. The 1 percent is if you're in law enforcement or the military and in the course of performing your duties, you come across an armed perpetrator. Or you're a licensed gun owner defending yourself, home, or family from an intruder.

In almost every case of murder, there is one of three common denominators that puts the victim in play and gives the killer the motivation they need to commit their heinous crime.

Money

Some people believe money is the root of all evil. Let's face it, unless you're living an ascetic lifestyle or are living it up, wearing sandals in a commune with no electricity, we all need money. Money buys freedom and the more of it you have, the more things you can do or obtain. The more money you have, the better the chance of living a fruitful life. Most of us will agree on that, unless of course you're a happy communist and in that case, you are in the wrong country because we all want to live the American dream.

We all want a large house in a great neighborhood, 2 cars, health insurance, and financial stability. Throw in 2 vacations a year, and enough of a cash cushion to fix the roof or update the house when your spouse gets bored with the aesthetics.

Sounds like Renton after he goes straight in Trainspotting. We all should strive to live a better life through good old fashion hard work. The problem with money is when folks take shortcuts to obtain it.

Man has been ripping off his brother from the beginning of time. When Cain got jealous of Abel, he whacked him out. When someone wants what you have and they are willing to take it through force, it can get ugly very fast. Depending on circumstances combined with your adversary's lack of conscious, a person's life can end in a split second.

Hold ups, car jackings, and home invasions, the list of violent crimes motivated by money seems to have no end. I don't think I have to beat you over the head by listing every crime, but you get the idea. There are some very bad people in this world whose mindset it is to take what you have through violence, and if your life just so happens to get in the way, so be it.

How many times have you been in a store somewhere waiting in line when some schmuck pulls out a wad of cash that could choke a horse? You can't pay for a new car or boat in cash anymore without setting off bells and whistles at the IRS, but this schmuck who's buying pampers is making it rain. Big Spender should be wearing a sandwich board that reads "Rob Me" on the front and back. Has this jerkoff not heard of a debit card?

It comes down to the old adage, "Why does a dog lick his balls?" Because he can, of course. In his mind, having the money is not good enough; he wants everybody in the world to know it. It's the "Hey look at me, I'm important" syndrome, also known as "the ugly American" or translated into Latin and Hebrew, "Flashus Cashus Schmuckus". Laying low is not in Flashy's repertoire.

Even if Flashy is a licensed gun owner, he's still giving some scumbag waiting in line 3 people behind the motivation to size him up and follow him to his car when he flashes that wad of cash. Flashy is now being stalked and he doesn't even know it. I'm all for having money, you just don't have to tell anyone who will listen that you have it.

Common sense things your parents should have taught you like being aware of your surroundings, can lower your chances of being the victim of a violent crime. Where you live or hang out can also affect your chances of being murdered. Avoiding areas where police sirens and gunshots are the norm would be a good start.

If you're on vacation in an unfamiliar place, do not stay out too late. If you're traveling on the road, get to your hotel before nightfall. You do not know the lay of the land but people lying in wait do, so try to get in for the night when you have the advantage of traveling in daylight.

Criminals typically do not work 9 to 5 jobs. They like to sleep in and work evenings. If you have something menial and not pressing to do, do it in the daylight. When my then 17 year old cousin obtained her driver's license, I sat her down and explained to her that she now had to think before she went somewhere at night in her car.

"Don't decide to vacuum your car at 11pm in a 7/11 parking lot on your way home from your girlfriend's house" I explained to her. "That's where you're going to get approached by someone looking to do you harm".

Who you associate with can also play a factor in getting murdered. Graciously decline dinner invitations from El Chapo

Guzman or other miscreants that can bring you trouble. If you're hanging out with your buddy who owes money to the wrong people, when they come to collect, tag, you're it too. You're just as big of a scumbag as he is as far as they are concerned. "In for a penny, in for a pound".

If you're meeting a stranger either through Craigslist or one of those dating websites, meet in a well-lit public place. Get there early and try to park as close to the meeting place as you can. You want to be able to get in and out as quickly as possible. Meeting a stranger in an alley, methadone clinic, or airport parking lot will usually ensure you will never be heard from again.

Low Key Is The Key

Take steps to insulate yourself from the risk of a robbery or burglary. If you are going to have work done on your home, choose a reputable company. Play it smart and hire someone who has as much to lose as you do.

Trying to save a few bucks by choosing a hillbilly handyman who does not carry liability insurance or a sign on his truck could get you hurt down the road. If you don't like the looks of someone who comes to your home to do work, you don't have to let them in. Tell them you have an emergency and will reschedule at a later date. Don't worry about hurting his feelings, he's probably a criminal, believe me he will understand why you didn't let him in.

Why risk the possibility of having some dirt bag you don't feel right about casing your home? He very well could be planning to make an unexpected visit at a later date. Or maybe he could be passing on to his friends the heads up about your valuables, security system, and how many people live there for a burglary down the road.

Wearing a lot of jewelry is another way to draw flies to a barbeque.

I understand every once in a while you want to dress up and look nice. The Academy Awards red carpet walk only comes once a year and you have to look your best or ~~Joan Rivers~~ (oops, see medical chapter) Melissa Rivers will tear you up. Wearing jewelry to a wedding or social event is one thing. Wearing a Rolex to a rap concert, laundromat, or dice game is another.

The Insult

Yes, something as simple as an insult or even a perceived insult can get you killed. From road rage to stepping on some drunk's foot in an upscale titty bar, violence can erupt into a split second catastrophe.

Unfortunately there's a portion of the population that goes around just looking to be insulted. The happy go lucky guy who can't wait to smash someone in the teeth. He's one beer away from being a fugitive again and is just looking for someone to cross that line to make an example of.

Accidentally cut this guy off with your car and you will feel his wrath. It was totally unintentional and you wave sorry to him in the rear view mirror hoping he understands it was just an accident. This guy however does not believe in accidents, he believes in on purposes. He isn't looking for a Whitman sampler from CVS, he wants blood and more importantly, he now wants yours.

You didn't wake up today anticipating playing bumper cars in your Hyundai against this lunatic. While Road Rage Ray chases you at high speeds yelling obscenities, you attempt to break every traffic law imaginable in hopes of getting the attention of a cop to pull you over to stop the madness. You think to yourself, "What did I do to this guy?" The answer is not much. You made the mistake of getting in his way and you must now be punished.

The same rule applies if you're unlucky enough to be in a bar with this guy and make the mistake of looking at him a split second too long or, God forbid, you spill a drink on him. He is going to call you out on it and he's not looking for your apology. He is just looking to let off a little steam, on your head!

When a situation like this arises, try to live in the real world and don't be so naive. You are in serious danger and should get away from this psycho immediately. Don't be a dickhead or the "I have the right of way" guy, who insists on crossing a street because you have the walk sign flashing, despite the fact a semi-truck is bearing down on you. Yes, you had the right of way and that will be duly noted when your family collects your death settlement.

I know he is not supposed to take your indiscretion this far, but he has. Don't be smug and say to yourself, "What's he going to do? Hit me?" Yes he is going to hit you, multiple times with a beer mug until you do not get off that filthy sawdust caked floor.

He is not worried about getting arrested for kicking your ass. As a matter of fact, he has been looking forward to it. Hell, he just saw his parole officer today and got a gold star for pissing into a cup. He is not worried about you suing him for damages either. What are you going to get from him in a lawsuit anyway? His twenty year old pickup truck, belt buckle, or prized Dale Earnhardt autographed radial tire?

He's not seeing you as the mild mannered engineer that you really are. He has no idea you wear a pocket saver at work, or that you care about the environment and sort your garbage every week. Right now he sees you as his ex-wife, the guy who fucked his ex-wife, or the local clergy who molested him way back when.

Either way, you have passed the point of no return and nothing you can say or do will get you out of this mess. He's looking to hurt you, plain and simple. Now at the very least, you're probably going to get your ass kicked, or worst case scenario, possibly killed.

While you're lying on the filthy floor getting stomped on by his motorcycle boots, you should be saying to yourself, "Didn't I go through this as a child? Shouldn't this part of my life, fighting with people be over?" You're right, you really shouldn't be lying on the floor playing possum, hoping he will stop and go away.

Hopefully you covered your head just enough to avoid permanent brain damage, and you should consider yourself lucky if you escape with a slight speech impediment or mild case of bed wetting.

More people get themselves killed because they do not sense a direct threat or know their surroundings. Being a decent guy not looking for trouble can work against you because you cannot comprehend what some sick fuck has going on in his head.

What did your father tell you, or should have told you, when you were a child? No matter how tough you are, there is always someone else out there who is a lot tougher. A guy in a bar who is looking for trouble has a temper that can go from 0 to 60 in a split second, and your life means nothing to him. Unfortunately for the civilized folks not looking for trouble, there are a lot of bad people out there with hair triggers just itching to hurt someone.

These people are looking to be insulted. If you're unlucky enough to cross their path, try to defuse the situation. Suck it up and apologize profusely and offer to buy them a beer. Who cares if he calls you a pussy. The cost of a flat tap beer might just save your teeth. He has nothing to lose except the autographed Dale Earnhardt radial, but you have everything in the world to lose, up to and including your life. In that split second, you have entered his world and if you're a decent guy, you are way in over your head. You are now playing by his rules, or lack thereof.

Avoid dangerous people and situations at all costs. For example, that bar you've never been to before, with the line of motorcycles parked outside and grown men wearing leather jackets with patches on the back should be avoided.

Challenging a stranger with tear drop tattoos on his face to a friendly game of pool is pushing the envelope a little. If he says yes, you better let him win. If you're dumb enough to be in one of these places and the shit hits the fan, run like hell. If you've had hip replacement surgery, you're not running anywhere.

Hopefully you have a carry permit and live in a state that has a stand your ground law. I am not advocating turning into Paul Kersey and going out to look for trouble. But a person does have the right to defend himself from dickheads looking to do them harm. I cannot stress enough, do not arm yourself and then go looking for trouble. Now go back to Walmart and return the Abraham Lincoln mask and baseball bat you purchased to right society's wrongs. Hopefully you saved the receipt and I maybe have saved your life.

It doesn't even have to be a total stranger you need to be careful of insulting, because someone you know can just as easily get offended and take your life. Sometimes knowing the person makes it that much more personal, as bad blood between two parties can build up for years to an unfortunate boiling point. Neighbors, coworkers, and business partners can cross the point of no return when they perceive they have either been humiliated or pushed too far.

The guy at work whose balls you've been breaking should really be left alone. There is a reason he brown bags it to work and eats alone in the lunchroom every day. He's antisocial and has been the punch line of jokes since kindergarten. He's like a dented can of tomato sauce that you grab off the shelf at your local grocery store. There's something wrong with it so you put it back and grab another one. You don't purchase and cook it risking giving everyone in your house the runs. Would your mother ever buy a dented can of sauce? Put the damn can back on the shelf and move on.

Every day, after breaking this guy's balls, you go home to your family never giving it a second thought. The problem is that he *is*, replaying the teasing in his mind over and over again. This guy is going home every day, mumbling to himself and motherfuckering you to the point that you're the only thing he's thinking about. You wanted his attention, now you have it and you have become the focal point of his life because he obsesses over getting even with you.

After he's had enough, he is going to go postal on your ass not worrying about delivering Christmas cards or catalogs during the holiday season. You're not a kid anymore, if you're breaking someone's balls and they aren't laughing, move on to someone who gets your humor. Don't be the bully who now has to look over both shoulders when he opens the garage door every morning hoping to avoid Jack Ruby on the way to work.

When I was a kid, there was a mild mannered guy with a lazy eye who owned a printing shop in my neighborhood. A slightly built unassuming guy, he seemed nice enough. In the winter we would shovel snow in front of his store for extra cash. He went on to purchase more properties around the neighborhood and was on his way to becoming a successful businessman. He became involved in a nasty legal dispute over a building with a local doctor that turned violent one day.

While their case pended in civil court, the doctor went into the printer's office and a heated argument ensued. I don't have first-hand knowledge of exactly what happened in that office that day. But what I do know is there was an argument and somehow the doctor knocked the printer's glass eye out of his head before leaving. Shaken, embarrassed, and humiliated, the printer pulled a gun from his desk, followed the fleeing doctor down a flight of stairs and confronted him outside.

After a brief exchange of words, he shot and killed the doctor. The printer was convicted of manslaughter but his case was later overturned by the appellate division thus setting him free. There is only his version of the story so it's hard to draw a sound conclusion of what really happened that day.

What we do know for sure is two men who were previously friendly and had done business together became adversaries, resulting in a man's death. They originally went about it the right way, trying to settle their differences legally. The case was already pending in court, so what was so important that had to be said in that office that day? Given the amount of education it takes to become a physician, one would suspect a doctor to be an educated, rational person. I'm guessing knocking a glass eye out of someone's head violates the Hippocratic Oath and goes against everything one would learn in medical school.

Was the printer that scared of the doctor that he thought he might come back and finish him off at a later date? Although he did catch a beating, he was still conscious enough to grab a gun and pursue the doctor outside and kill him. Had he just called the police, he would have had the world by the balls. He surely would have won the property case not to mention he could've sued the balls off the doctor and have him arrested for kicking his ass. What jury isn't going to side with a guy who had a glass marble punched out of his head? He could have afforded the best Ocularist money could buy.

But he let the beating get the better of him, took the doctor's life and changed his own forever. He did eventually beat the case but at what cost? He was arrested and almost sent to prison with his name splashed across the news. For Christ sakes thirty years later here I am bringing it up all over again. I am sure he incurred great legal costs to defend and later appeal his case. He wasn't a career criminal so he had to be stressing about going to prison. People from my neighborhood will always remember him as a murderer. He should have let it go.

I have arrested men who have killed multiple times before, and never in a million years would I have thought that meek guy who owned the print shop could take a life. You never really know what is going on in someone's mind, nor do you know what they are capable of.

Love

"Love is a fog that burns with the first daylight of reality" Charles Bukowski

I saved the best for last because love can drive the sane to insane in a split second. "The Power of Love" is not just a Huey Lewis song, it's a very real and very powerful emotion and if you're not careful choosing your partner, it just might get you killed.

Love is wonderful, isn't it? I mean who doesn't like being in love? Everything is wonderful when you have your rose colored glasses on. The birds are singing and everything is coming up roses. When we are first hit with cupid's arrow, we never seem to see our new lover's faults and if we do, we ignore or excuse them. Farting, belching, and leaving the toilet seat up are all ignored as we are oblivious to our new mate's shortcomings.

A few years ago, a buddy and I were looking into buying a business which at first glance, looked like a really lucrative deal. On paper it looked like a wonderful cash business in a great location. But as we further negotiated the deal with the seller, something didn't seem right.

He was very vague about the finances of the business and did not seem forthcoming with many of the questions we asked.

The detective in me smelled a rat. I went to town hall and pulled public records of the business and found out not only were the sellers lying to us about a litany of things, but they couldn't sell the business as a result of a pending lawsuit. We were disappointed to say the least and the deal fell apart.

My buddy groused and said to me, "This sucks, we really could have made it work. Maybe we should still try? " And so he started rationalizing a way to make the deal work despite the fact it had so many problems and the sellers were scumbags.

"Do you know who you sound like?" I asked. "You sound like a guy who has fallen for a beautiful woman loaded with problems".

"What are you talking about?" he asked. "Let me give you an example", I said.

Did you know she filed for bankruptcy and stole from her family? Yes, but she's beautiful.

Did you know her ex-husband just got out of prison and has sworn to kill anybody who is dating her? But she's beautiful.

Did you know she has hepatitis A, B and C, AIDS and oh, by the way, a slight Heroin addiction? But she's beautiful.

Needless to say he got the point and stopped hounding me about purchasing the business.

People will justify anything if they really want something bad enough, despite the fact that it could be hazardous to their health. They will overlook a red flag the size of a bull fighter's cape waving in their face if they covet something bad enough, especially someone they are attracted to. For men, it's called thinking with your dick. For women it's called… well, what is it called? Anyway you get the drift.

Sleeping With The Enemy

Choosing a stable partner is the key to a healthy, thriving relationship. It's a lot easier said than done. I don't want to sound like a Lifetime television movie starring Meredith Baxter Birney depicting a battered woman who refuses to press charges against her hillbilly husband, but there is some truth in those movies. If your partner starts hitting you, they are not going to stop. It's only going to get worse until he or she gets tired of hitting you, or they kill you. Those are your options and neither is good. Why on earth would you want to sleep with one eye open and the other swollen shut?

It's not like domestic violence is a new phenomenon sweeping the country like Snapchat. Unfortunately it's been around for years and it doesn't appear to be coming to an end anytime soon. If your significant other's way of showing how much they care about you is a bitch slap, you really should get away from them quickly. Don't worry about your clothes or your coveted magnet collection on the refrigerator that holds the post-it notes reminding them not to hit you, just get the hell out of there.

There is so much information out there about the dangers of domestic violence; it's unimaginable why someone would actually hang around for a second helping. The "He hits me because he loves me" logic just doesn't hold up. Can you imagine if he really loved you? What would he do then for an encore? How can you proclaim to love, or even like someone and then treat their face like a punching bag?

Avoid someone who is already involved or married. This seems pretty simple, right? Nothing will get someone's blood pressure up faster than finding out their significant other is cheating on them. It can make a law abiding citizen go postal.

Taking something that doesn't belong to you can get you killed. Forget about sharing someone in a relationship. For those of you hippies left over from the 1960s, it's over, there is no more free love or free lunch for that matter so grow up and get over it. Shave, cut your ponytail, and join the rest of society.

Love can be the trifecta in the murder category because if someone catches you sleeping with his or her spouse, it may have just triggered the wrath of all 3 murder components. Think about it, a guy catches you screwing his wife. He now has lost his love. It's definitely an insult because now he realizes he's been in the dark and lied to for who knows how long. He is definitely embarrassed because when friends and family find out about the affair, it makes it more difficult to keep the relationship together. Nobody likes to lose face and it's a humiliating thing to live with or have to explain to your peers.

If you're headed to divorce court, it may be costly dividing assets. Every divorce ends with someone getting fucked over. What you did or the attorney you hire will determine who is the fucker and who is the fuckee. Getting martinized by your ex-spouse and their attorney may leave you living like a roach.

I'm not claiming to have the same sharp insight as the horse tooth jackass internet dating guru who claims his website will help you find a mate. Rather I would like to provide you with a guide of dating warning signs to avoid when finding a partner.

What women should avoid:

- His favorite movie is Sleeping With The Enemy.
- He carries a baseball bat in his car at all times, but doesn't play softball.
- Recently retired from the UFC circuit.
- Thinks a wife beater is a dinner jacket.
- Drinks Chai Tea Latte (not dangerous, just a douche-bag)
- Owns a pickup truck with bumper stickers and mud splashed on the side.
- Is an Islamic radical who makes unusual purchases with your debit card.
- Mullets.
- Facial tattoos.
- Drives a 1980s muscle car.

What men should avoid:

- Soup heads.
- Compulsively texts her ex-boyfriend during a dinner you're paying for.
- The headliner of her car has cigarette burns.
- Has men's underwear with skid marks lying around her apartment.
- She consumes alcohol during pregnancy and you're not the father.
- Tattoos with spelling mistakes.
- Unannounced visits to your home after 1am.
- Favorite is movie *Fatal Attraction*

- Dances on tables at a club near the airport.
- Bad credit.

Dating or marrying the mentally unstable can be quite challenging. If you must date the mentally unstable, try not to leave firearms or sharp objects lying around when they are visiting.

Sometimes their parents will do you a favor and brand them with a name that should give you a heads up that they are crazy. Women named after weather patterns, moon phases, or names that end in i (Storm, Eclipse, Destini, etc.), and men named after animals or Greek mythology characters (Colt, Satyr, Thor, etc.) should be avoided at all costs.

If they ever mention the phrase “I would kill you” in a conversation, it’s time to run and not walk. They might be a lot of fun at first but you will enter a nightmare at some point. Try to avoid burned out booze hounds whose asses are screwed into bar stools because someday you just might get hit in the head with that stool.

Your chances of dying by murder are pretty slim if you live by the golden rule, choose a stable mate, and try not to live in a demilitarized zone. Don’t keep late hours, and never take what does not belong to you. Follow these suggestions and you should avoid being murdered.

Chapter 7

Suicide Is Not Painless

When I was in my twenties, my friends and I drove to Florida for spring break. We were having a blast when I made the mistake of asking one of my friends who didn't seem to be having a good time what was wrong.

"What's the difference, we're all going to die anyway" he said.

"What an asshole", I thought to myself. Here we are in the prime of our lives with no responsibility, having a good time in the sunshine state and this fucking guy drags a dead dog into the room.

I was too young and selfish to understand this guy was seriously depressed. I just couldn't understand his mindset. As a matter of fact, looking back he was always depressed and often talked about dying. We probably should have tried to get him professional help, but we were unequipped to handle the situation ourselves.

When we hit our thirties, we went our separate ways as a lot of childhood friends do. To date, I know that he hasn't committed suicide because I look him up online periodically. I hope he is okay and I wish him well, I just don't feel the need to reconnect with him at this point because he would depress me.

As a matter of fact, at this stage of my life I probably couldn't be in the same room with him for more than five minutes. I guess that says a lot about me. I could never be a psychiatrist or bartender because I don't like listening to other people's misery or problems.

Unfortunately we are all born to die and in this chapter we will cover those who willingly jump to the front of the line.

At one time or another, probably everyone has contemplated suicide. How far you want to take that thought is entirely up to you. I guess everyone had their reasons, but are they good reasons? As fucked up as this world is now, how bad is it really? If you are reading this book, I'm pretty sure you have four walls, electricity, and a refrigerator. You even have discretionary income to buy this stupid book, right?

You're not in a cave somewhere, hiding from guys dressed in black looking to saw your head off with a bread knife to make propaganda videos, are you? Diseases like polio and smallpox, which would have eradicated cities in the past, have now almost been wiped off the face of the earth.

Life expectancy has been continually going upward. When people sneezed in days of old and someone said "God bless you", they really meant it. When someone became ill in the old days it was taken quite seriously. Cavemen evicted the sick from their caves in an effort to save the clan. They may have had pink asses, but they weren't stupid. During outbreaks of typhoid and the plague, villagers burned the mattresses and linens of the sick just to be sure the disease wouldn't spread. Typhoid Mary, who exposed countless families to typhoid fever, spent the rest of her life in exile because she refused to stop cooking and cleaning for people. People pissed and crapped in their own water sources spreading cholera and dysentery.

Science and technology have not only extended our life expectancy, but have enabled us to look better too. Chances are if you take good care of yourself, you will age better. Even if you don't take care of yourself but are still vain enough, there are plenty of products and treatments to make you look good.

There is no end to the amount of things you can get done to raise your self-esteem. Overweight? No problem, they can tie your stomach or suck the fat right out of your ass with a vacuum. Not happy with your teeth? Have them straightened or bleached at the shopping mall while your kids play at the Apple Store. That'll give you the Kardashian smile you've always wanted. Flat chested? You can have your tits inflated to the PSI of your liking. There are facelifts to chase away crows' feet while stitching a smile on your face that will never come off.

We have pills that do everything from weight loss to making your dick work. There is no end in sight to the amount of products and procedures designed to make us feel better about ourselves. If you can put off killing yourself another week, you can get your hands on the new Apple watch that's coming out!!

Some will commit suicide quickly, not wanting to be talked out of it by friends or family because they are not looking for feedback. Some will do strategic planning, taking the time to write a letter to loved ones saying their goodbyes and getting their affairs in order before executing their final plan.

I knew a guy who took the time to mail out his goodbye letters to loved ones and waited a few days until the letters arrived before he committed suicide. I was perplexed because I'm sure he debated the issue over the course of those few days. You would think that since he gave himself a grace period during the time those letters were in transit to reflect about the consequences of what was to come, he would have changed his mind. I guess in his mind once those letters were mailed, there was no turning back.

Maybe the shame and embarrassment of facing friends and family who had read the letters was too much for him to bear. I wonder if he took the time to send those letters as a way of locking himself in. One thing's for sure, and that is you will never know what is going on in someone's mind, especially the mindset of someone who is suicidal. A problem that may seem infinitesimal to you may be the end of the world to that person, and be the motivation for someone to take their own life.

Most people will get a hold of themselves somehow, maybe talk to loved ones, seek professional help, or are just able to pull themselves out of the spiraling nose dive they are in. But if you have the balls to check out and commit suicide, that's it, game over, no mas, thank you for playing Nintendo, you're gone.

I am lapsed Catholic and would like to put the finality of death into perspective while giving you a Sunday school class at the same time. Every spring, Christians celebrate the holiday of Easter or the Resurrection of Jesus Christ, which commemorates his rise from the dead. After suffering a painful death by crucifixion, Christ was entombed in a cave sealed with a boulder. 3 days later, the boulder moved, and the cave was empty as Jesus Christ rose from the dead and proceeded to make several appearances to his disciples. Other than JC, and that's up for debate, nobody else has been able to pull off that trick since.

Alright, even though he was spotted in shopping malls as chronicled by the National Enquirer, Elvis has not made it back from the great beyond. Of all the wonderful medical advances we now enjoy, bringing people back from the dead is not one of them. My mother's "death is so final" quote pretty much sums it all up. After you die, there is nobody to go see or complain to, at least not in this world.

My upbringing taught there's a heaven, although I am not sure. I'm certainly not going to fast track the world that I know exists, for one that may not. I'm not leaving this world until my body and mind give out and even then, I'm going out kicking and screaming.

Let's say the Christian brothers with the big fists at St. Raymond's were right and there is a heaven waiting for us at the end of our lives. Hopefully the pearly gates will have short lines and everybody is having a good time yucking it up with Saint Peter.

I'm hoping if and when I get up there, St. Peter is in a great mood and can't locate my file so that I get in on a technicality. Maybe it's like the playboy mansion and God is a gracious host and not a creepy letch like Heff. Maybe heaven is a nonstop cocktail party with free food and drink where you get to schmooze with the famous celebrities who have passed on.

Imagine getting to heaven and fifteen minutes in, you're already invited to a debaucherous Tyco cocktail party. You're enjoying Liberace playing the piano when TV pitchman Billy Maze jumps in your grill and tries to sell you some Oxiclean. You try to blow him off, but he won't take no for an answer. He tells you that here in heaven everyone wears white and this is a must have product. When you ask him about the white powdery substance under his nose, he changes the subject and tells you Oxiclean also gets out sins! I have often wondered if you were an asshole in this world, if you would still be an asshole in heaven.

After enjoying a few pigs in a blanket (no heartburn in heaven pal), you notice *the* Elvis Presley off in a corner talking to Michael Jackson. You think, "how great is this, I get to meet two kings", as you make your way over and try to ease your way into their conversation. Then you get within earshot and you realize Elvis is pissed and choking the shit out of Michael Jackson for marrying his daughter, Lisa Marie.

"MJ is not going to moonwalk his way out of this one", you say to yourself. Just as Elvis threatens to shove one of his blue suede shoes up the king of pop's ass, you interject.

"King, that was years ago, we're in heaven now, let bygones be bygones". Elvis spins around with the flying kick he could only do in the early Vegas years. His TCB chain almost hits your chin and you smell mesquite barbecue on his breath.

Just as you're about to compliment him on his gold diamond encrusted jumpsuit, the king tells you to mind your own business and to get the fuck away from him in his soothing voice. As you're ushered away by Colonel Tom Parker and the Dixie mafia you say to yourself, "What an asshole, he ruined it for me" and "I wish I never met him".

You swear you will never download his music again, and then you realize you're dead and there are no illegal downloads in heaven. After calming down, you come to your senses and realize a father wants what's best for his daughter, even in heaven.

But what if there is no perfect afterlife? No heaven, no nothing. What if we are like computers in that after they break down they are thrown away? Maybe Jack Nicholson was right in "As Good As It Gets", and life is about sailboats and noodle salad. Maybe this is it and we're stuck with the dickheads on earth with no other place to ascend to. Are you willing to trade the life you know for something that may not exist?

My dad passed away eight years ago and he was the biggest ball buster of all time. Trust me, if he could sneak out of heaven or wherever he is for 30 seconds and come back to this world to bust my balls, it would have happened already.

But there is good news; suicide is the one category in this book that's totally avoidable. Unless you're the poor bastard who gets taken out by some douchebag who wants the company, like a suicide bomber, it's pretty avoidable. In the case of the suicide bomber, it's called murder by asshole. Unlike other chapters in this book where it's either stupidity, being at the wrong place at the wrong time, or long term systematic pattern of ignoring a healthy lifestyle, all you have to do is *not kill yourself.*

The name and lyrics of the song from the hit 1970s movie and TV show *M*A*S*H*, "Suicide Is Painless", is factually incorrect. How does anyone know in the split second, no matter what method you choose to kill yourself, that it's not painful?

Shooting yourself, taking a bottle of sleeping pills, or throwing yourself in front of an Amtrak train cannot be pleasant. Life leaving your mind and body cannot be a good feeling. Not to mention the mess you left behind, like Alanis Morissette sings.

You don't want to be a bother to anyone so you take your own life. Ever give it some thought that someone close to you is going to find your body? Ever think of what that's going to do to them, jerk off? Somebody has to pay for your funeral, you deadbeat. Your family and friends will never get over it nor will they ever understand. Some may even feel responsible for your death and will carry that around with them for the rest of their lives. Give that some thought before you decide to check out, you inconsiderate selfish fuck.

Not that there is any reason for killing yourself, but killing yourself over love just defies logic. Here I go again with Huey Lewis singing about "The Power of Love", but it sums it all up. Love is a wonderful emotion, and just like sadness or fear, it's still an emotion. It's the best emotion obviously and being in love is wonderful.

It's intoxicating and seductive, but just like with any powerful drug, once you're off it, you can crash and go through a brutal withdrawal period. That's when problems begin. When you break up with someone you love, you feel like shit and you're not sleeping or eating for different reasons now. You go back and forth, should I call him or her, as you wrestle with your emotions to fish or cut bait.

Depression sets in like a gray cloudy November day in the northeast. Every song on the radio reminds you of him or her as you pray they will pick up the phone and call you. You're an open wound and everything that reminds you of them hurts. You feel yourself getting pulled down and nothing is fun anymore. Until you decide that enough is enough and you have to right this ship before you go down with it.

You call your friends for advice or meet up with them for happy hour. It's not really what you want to do but it's going to keep you busy and distracted. It's the equivalent of being really hungry and settling for shitty food, it will get you by for now. Idle hands are the devil's workshop so it's better to go out with friends than to sit around dwelling about your lousy break up. Unless you're Charles Manson, your friends will take your side and tell you what a piece of shit your ex was.

They will all tell you that you don't need him or her, and that you deserve better. All of a sudden you're hearing, "We never liked him" which you cannot comprehend. How can this be? My friends never liked him? It starts to dawn on you that maybe they are right about your ex and you bet on the wrong horse.

As you digest the shitty food (a.k.a. your friends' advice), it slowly but surely begins to sink in. As time goes by, your open wound begins to heal. When the wound closes, you will develop a scar. Some scars are visible and some aren't but rest assured there will be a scar for a while. Some heal faster than others and some will never heal completely. The wound heals just enough to go on with life and you say you will never give love a second chance, although you ultimately will.

If you're toying around with the idea of committing suicide because your girlfriend or husband has left you, stop right there. Nobody and I mean nobody is worth killing yourself over. My dad would tell me after I got dumped by some chick to stop feeling sorry for myself.

"Women are like buses and there will be another one coming by shortly" he would say, and the same applies to men.

The internet has made dating like the Wild West and it's easier than ever to meet new people. There are lonely people out there waiting to hear from you. You can and will meet someone else because there is an ass for every seat. I know I'm on my soap box preaching like some banana fingered self-help guru, but again, nobody is worth killing yourself over.

If you're not going to take my advice and are hell bent on killing yourself, please do it alone. Don't be the asshole who feels compelled to bring somebody else with you for the ride. Suicide means to kill oneself and it's not a team effort. It always amazed me that someone is so miserable enough to kill themselves yet want company on the way out.

Jerk offs like terrorists or those who snap and go on a shooting spree in shopping malls killing strangers. They want out of this life and want to take innocent people with them. They have no connection to their victims, choosing them and the location because of their own twisted agenda. They feel no remorse and it must bring them some perverse pleasure playing God and ending some poor soul's life. I'm guessing in some twisted way, they want to be remembered as scumbags for all of eternity.

Others know their poor victims quite well. Ex-lovers, supervisors, neighbors, or whoever else they feel have done them wrong. In their mind they have no reason to live and those responsible for their misery must pay and pay dearly. They are in so much pain and they want those they perceive responsible to feel the same pain. If it wasn't bad enough that they are going to take some poor person's life, they usually make sure the victim sees them coming.

I really do not know if there is a hell after this life. The Christian brothers at my high school said there is but who really knows? If there is a hell, it should be reserved for those who take their own lives while taking some poor innocent victim along with them for the ride. Hopefully when those selfish fucks get down there, someone who resembles the character on a can of deviled ham is waiting for them, to shove a hot poker up their ass for all eternity.

The only 2 things I honestly think would make me seriously consider suicide are terminal cancer, or a very long prison sentence. All my life I have tried not to paint myself into a corner and both of those scenarios seem bleak with no way out. Either way you're going to die a terrible death, physically and mentally.

This book is not meant to be depressing and I hope I didn't drag a dead dog into your living room like my former friend would often do. If I did, I am truly sorry. Right about now you should start hearing "Always Look on the Bright Side of Life" by Monty Python in your head.

Chapter 8

Places To Avoid

I should have named this chapter "Why can't we just stay home?" because time and time again we insist on going to places that are hazardous to our health. Large crowds or remote locations usually equal dangerous activity where all hell can break loose at a moment's notice. It's as if we have no idea how vulnerable we are in this dangerous world we inhabit. Visiting third world countries to take photos or dropping acid at a Burning Man gathering is playing Russian roulette with your life. I'm not anti-travel or advocating living like my aunt who never leaves her house. But you have to be cognizant of your surroundings and weigh the risks of traveling to places that are dangerous.

I would rather watch the Travel Channel from the safety of my home than go somewhere looking for a good place to die. Like my father would say, "if you go looking for trouble, you're going to find it", and these are some places to find it.

Anywhere after 11 pm

I was 21 years old, living at home without a care in the world. After being out all night feeling immortal, I came through the door and ran into my father who was on his way to work. It was around 4am and he knew I had been out all night drinking.

He said to me with disgust in his voice, "Nothing good can happen after 11pm". I just nodded because there really wasn't much to say to my poor father who was on his way to another day of back breaking work. Going up the stairs to my room I had a moment of clarity.

Something wasn't fair in this scenario. I had the world by the balls, I was young with a civil service job, living at home and staying out all night and here's my poor father dragging his ass to work in a meat freezer. Maybe he was right? 4am is not the time to have a deep heart to heart discussion with your father about staying out all night drinking. But then again, my dad did have a way to make his point without having to beat you over the head with it.

The reality is nothing good does happen after 11pm, no matter where you are. That last drink you just had to have can cost you a DUI or a lot worse. Even if you're sober as a judge and the designated driver for the night, you can still get hit by another drunk on the road.

There are only 3 kinds of people on the road after 11pm;

cops, cabs, and drunks. Even if you're not drunk, you still don't want to run into two out of the three. The later it gets, the chances of a fight breaking out in a club or bar increase quite a bit. I don't know about you but I can think of better things to do on a Saturday night than get hit by a chair or stray bullet.

If you're out drinking and driving, your odds of getting pulled over by the cops increase tenfold after 11pm. The midnight shift has just come on for the night and they are full of piss and vinegar. There are fewer cars on the road (or fish in the stream) to distract the cops.

Your burned out tail light probably wouldn't have been noticed at 9pm with the amount of traffic on the road. Cops get bored like anyone else sitting in a car all night and might want to stretch their legs at your expense.

At 2am they definitely will notice your tail light out, and tag, you're it. Those three extra hours at the bar are going to cost you a few thousand dollars for the DUI, plus the cost of the tail light.

I knew a guy who was a great cop and all around nice guy. He had one drink too many one night and killed a woman with his car in the early morning hours on his way home. He lost his career and has to live forever with the guilt of having taken a person's life. On top of that he was sentenced to several years in prison which is the last place in the world an ex-cop would want to be.

I did plenty of stupid things when I was young, and put myself in places and situations that could have ended my life long before I became a police officer. As I grew older, I became more aware of my surroundings and situations. To survive as a cop, it is critical to know exactly where you are, and more importantly how to exit in an instant. Where you are can be just as dangerous as what you are doing.

Criminals are not 9 to 5 type of people and love to work nights. The cover of darkness is their best friend and affords them a security blanket. Your chances of becoming the victim of a crime go up considerably after dark. There are fewer cops and witnesses around, but certainly more criminals and that does not swing the odds of safety in your favor.

On the off chance you're under 30 and reading this book, I hope I saved you some money and trouble. If you are over 30, you probably should know better than to stay out all night living a debaucherous lifestyle, but if you don't know, good luck to you because you're going to need it.

Hospitals and Germs

I'm not a big fan of germs so the last place I want to be is in a hospital. I take extraordinary and sometimes paranoid steps to avoid hospitals at all costs. Hell, if I can get out of visiting someone in the hospital, I will.

Famous bank robber Willie Sutton was once asked why he chose banks to rob. His answer was, "Because that's where the money is". My mantra to living a healthy life is avoiding hospitals because "that's where the germs are". When I was a police officer I sometimes had to spend hours at a time in hospitals, guarding sick or injured prisoners. Every time it seemed like an eternity. Whenever I touched something in a hospital, I found myself scrubbing my hands in the sink like Lady Macbeth, trying to cleanse the blood off my hands.

We are lucky to be living in these modern times with all the advances in medicine. Although sometimes there are those who go into the hospital for a simple procedure and will come out with something a lot worse, provided they come out at all. The over prescribing of antibiotics has produced terminator-like germs that cause all sorts of problems.

How about a simple case of the flesh eating bacteria that can transform your skin into looking like a first degree burn victim? I couldn't model socks but still, who is looking forward to a skin graft? How about the mad cow disease that makes you look like an asshole before you die?

Well, maybe you can't get the mad cow disease from a hospital unless they're serving beef from the UK with your Jell-O, but you get the point.

I'm sorry, but you can't tell me there aren't incompetent doctors and poorly run hospitals out there. I knew plenty of incompetent cops when I worked for the NYPD. Like the old joke says, "what do you call a guy who got the lowest passing grade on the medical board exam?" "Doctor"

Incompetent doctors and hospitals produce subpar surgeries. If you don't believe me, google what happened to comedian Dana Carvey. The poor guy went in for surgery to correct a blocked artery. When he awoke, he learned the doctor performed surgery on the wrong artery! The poor bastard had to go through a second procedure to repair the correct artery. I would have chased that doctor around the parking lot provided my blocked artery held up.

Hospitals should not be in the same league as your local mechanic who charges you for a complete brake job when he really only adjusted them. On the other side of the coin, you have hypochondriacs who love visiting doctors and hospitals, wasting everybody's time. They hound doctors for useless medications or unnecessary surgeries. If you're sick or need surgery by all means go to the hospital. What I could never understand were the schmucks who visit hospitals like going to a movie to kill time. The emergency room is the last place in the world anyone should want to visit. The odds are you're going leave the ER sicker than when you went in, provided you ever get out at all.

Flight travel has made it easy for people to go from continent to continent, bringing with them a whole host of diseases and bacteria from faraway lands. I am of the opinion that what happens in Vegas should stay in Vegas, and the same should apply to remote jungle locations. If you're living in the Congo reading this book and feel sick, please stay in your hut until you're feeling better because we don't want a pandemic here in the United States.

We send doctors and nurses to your country to treat your sick. We endure Sally Struthers begging us to sponsor your children for 50 cents a day, what more do you want from us? We have enough germs over here and don't want anymore.

Just ask those poor hospital workers in Houston a few years ago. They thought they were treating some poor guy with a bad case of the flu but before they knew it, they were exposed to the deadly Ebola virus. Ebola makes the flu look like a Disney feature.

Ebola causes you to melt through uncontrollable vomiting, diarrhea, and the occasional eye socket bleeding. If you're exposed to Ebola, you are put in quarantine in the hospital for a month without basic cable.

I feel like a three dollar whore when I leave the hospital, dirty and cheap. When I get home I shower immediately and burn my clothes in the back yard. There's not enough vitamin C or Airborne I can consume, awaiting the 3 day incubation period of cold symptoms after I grace a hospital.

Unless you're a hospital worker or really sick, you should really avoid hospitals. If you're a hypochondriac then by all means go, you deserve what you get.

Running With the Idiots in Pamplona, Spain

One way to experience jet lag, shorten your life, and receive inferior medical treatment all in one shot is to visit Pamplona, Spain and run with the bulls. I could never wrap my head around why United States citizens would fly to Spain and run in the streets with a bunch of bulls and village idiots for excitement. If you live in America and really want to run for your life, fly to NYC and ride the subway during rush hour. It's a lot cheaper and they speak English in the emergency room. Plus if you survive, you can catch a Broadway show afterwards.

Maybe you are consumed with the literary works of the great Ernest Hemingway. But just because you emulate the guy doesn't mean you have to walk or run in his footsteps. Taking advice from a guy who had accomplished so much only to put a shotgun in his mouth is not the way to go. Would you take sleeping advice from Michael Jackson?

I'm guessing there isn't a lot to do in Pamplona, or maybe it's overpopulated and this is a way to enforce survival of the fittest? Maybe getting gored by a bull in Spain is like getting a tattoo in the US, though I really don't want to do either. I don't want to sound like an elitist, but running down a narrow street with a bunch of angry bulls and foreigners dressed like they work in a pizzeria isn't my idea of a fun afternoon.

The bulls on the other hand must live for this shit. They spend their lives grazing and humping on a farm somewhere, except for 8 days in July when they receive parole. Then they get to run half a mile with an unlimited amount of idiots to trample without recourse. It's like a "Death Race 2000" for bulls.

Imagine the flight home with a hole in your side the size of a fist. They might not tell you, but trust me, your friends and family are going to think you are an idiot no matter how many times they ask you to tell them about your adventure in Spain. I equate running with the bulls to American football in the winter. I would much rather watch it on TV than be at the stadium.

Times Square on New Year's Eve

It amazes me that people love to congregate in large numbers with total strangers. You don't know these people or what they are capable of. Something goes wrong and you could be trampled in an instant. A lot can go wrong in a crowd and nothing personifies this more than New Year's Eve at Times Square in New York City, otherwise known as "the dickhead convention".

This is the last place in the world any cop wants to be. For twenty years, I was part of probably five thousand NYPD personnel required to work that night to keep order and try to make sure nobody got hurt. But inevitably, it does happen and it happens a lot. I never could comprehend why so many people would come from all over the world just to be uncomfortable.

For starters, it's December in New York so you're going to freeze your ass off. If you can see your breath and still go outside without a justifiable reason, you're a dickhead. People tend to get ballsy in crowds especially at night. So imagine the pack mentality of a dark crowd of about a million people who attend this event annually. I may be antisocial, but I cannot think of 30 people I would want to spend time with, let alone a million.

New Year's Eve is amateur hour complete with thousands of young and underage people with no life experience binge drinking at a place where things can get out of hand quickly. Those large crowds are corralled like cattle pushed into pens constructed of wooden sawhorse barriers. It looks orderly when shown from high above by Ryan Seacrest on TV. But in reality, there are a lot of miserable people trapped in those pens.

God forbid you have to use the bathroom that night, because the restaurants aren't going to let you use theirs. They've had their bathrooms trashed before, so you're out of luck. The good news is that if you're into golden showers, you're in luck because that's the night you're going to receive one whether you want it or not.

The "orderly crowd" shown on television is getting their pockets picked, felt up, or in some cases, changing tampons. People are stacked so close together. Someone will sometimes pass out standing up, only to slide down onto the street. Guess what happens when some lightweight who cannot hold his liquor decides to start vomiting uncontrollably inside the crowd? The pushing to get away from him begins and people are trampled. So if you're the type who likes his space and who doesn't always get along with his neighbors, you really should stay home that night.

An added bonus if you survive the initial New Year's Eve festivities is your journey home. While you were getting drunk yelling, screaming, and taking selfies, you were being sized up for slaughter.

You see, there are other people there that night who are as sober as the cops. They're called criminals and they are going to rob or beat the shit out of you as you try to get home. When the ball drops at midnight, the confetti falls like snow, making sanitation workers on overtime very happy. Hugs and sloppy kisses are given out like it's Woodstock.

Cops begin breaking down and stacking wooden barriers, hoping to get home to loved ones who have stayed up late to greet them after a long and exhausting shift. The massive crowd dissipates like steam in various directions with 95 percent of the crowd having had their fill and now wanting to go home.

But there are those who can never have enough of a good time. It's the guy who always has to stay for last call at the bar, or is the last to leave at every party. They continue to linger around obviously drunk taking photos and hugging everyone. They bring unwanted attention to themselves by yelling and stumbling around. While they are busy showing off their iPhone and cameras, the hyenas are patiently waiting for their prey in the shadows of the side streets. It's like watching "Animal Planet" live.

You see that the wounded gazelle (or stumbling drunkard in this case) must pass through the valley (or side streets) to get home. The problem is a pack of hyenas (or hood rats from the Bronx or Brooklyn) have sized them up and are lying in wait for them.

As the wounded gazelles pass through the side streets out of sight of their shepherds, they are slapped around and relieved of their valuables by their sober predators who then vanish like Houdini into thin air. Sometimes a victimized gazelle will run back to Times Square and into the arms of an unsympathetic cop, who after standing out in the cold with drunks for 12 hours, really doesn't want to hear their tales of woe.

You want to live longer and have a good time on New Year's Eve? Stay home with loved ones or go to a small party. The food is better and you can piss indoors. If you're afraid of driving drunk, get the Uber application on your smartphone, it's faster and cheaper than a cab.

Stay away from any large outdoor event on New Year's Eve, especially Times Square, unless of course you want to spend the night in a police station looking at mugshots.

Air Shows

What is the fascination with airshows? As I write this chapter, a plane crashed into a crowd at an airshow in the United Kingdom killing at least twenty. Air Shows are another dangerous thing of the past that people refuse to give up.

Air shows are held in the summer so you are going to sweat your balls off, slathering on the sunscreen, watching crop dusting fools zip by overhead. I'm guessing the pilots doing these stunts at air shows are weekend warriors, or whose skills have deteriorated to a large degree. I doubt an active 20 year pilot for American Airlines is going to jump into a world war biplane and terrorize a crowd of morons for shits and giggles over the county fairgrounds for the day. He has too much to lose to do something idiotic like that.

It's the guy who has too much money and time on his hands, whose hobby is going to get him and a crowd of dickheads killed. He wants to be a showoff, flying some idiotic contraption over the heads of countless idiots putting everyone's lives at risk. Did you ever stop to think that your last meal may be a corndog and a Prilosec before you're incinerated by a flying machine?

I understand people's fascination with danger, I really do. What I don't understand is why people have to get so close to danger to appreciate it. You can watch the same thing on television or YouTube. You don't have to stand in an open field waiting for the fireball overhead. Inevitably an engine goes out, power lines are hit, or they just feel like slamming into each other.

If you want inexpensive entertainment on a summer evening, visit a public boat ramp in Florida. When the boats return to the docks after a long hot day of drinking out on the water, that's when the fun begins.

Drunk and sunburned boat captains jockey for position to get their boats to the loading ramp first. You usually can only get one boat off at a time so the boats begin to bunch up, inevitably crashing into each other.

Watching fat bastards in wife beaters throwing haymakers at each other is endless fun. If you're lucky you may see a boat fall off its trailer or watch the cops take somebody to jail. You can sit and watch from the comfort of your air conditioned car, like a drive-in movie. There you won't have to worry about some moron in a plane crashing into you and burning you alive.

Cruise Ships

On a cruise ship, you can kick back and relax while getting rid of a loved one forever. How many times do we have to be warned by Greta Van Susteren not to get on a cruise ship? It seems like every time you turn on the television, someone has gone missing at sea on what has become a floating crime scene. Cruise ships are real life murder mystery dinner theater but with a better buffet.

They are the perfect place to get rid of that pain in the ass you have been married to for far too long. Hopefully you planned well and took out a sizeable life insurance policy on him or her. If you played your cards right, your insurance company won't ask too many questions before paying out on your missing spouse. It's the perfect crime really because the ocean is a great place to vanish without a trace, just ask Olivia Newton John's ex-boyfriend.

Most of the time on a cruise, everyone is drunk, having a good time and not paying attention to anything. If you can manage to push your spouse overboard without anyone seeing it, you're home free. The ship probably won't even stop, I mean who wants to break up a party? Maybe the DJ will make an announcement to ask if anyone heard a scream after playing "Hot, Hot Hot" for the third time, but he's not stopping the conga line.

When the ship docks at your Caribbean paradise, cry a lot and seek help from the village idiots who will do a half assed investigation on a mobile crime scene. Let the mascara run and don't forget to call your in laws to profess your love for your missing spouse. When you get back to the States, lawyer up and refuse to do any further interviews because you're going to be mentally exhausted from pondering where to spend the life insurance money.

If disappearing doesn't scare the shit out of you, how about the mysterious case of diarrhea that continues to haunt cruise ships? When the Norwalk virus comes a-knocking on a cruise ship, you're fucked. Imagine the worst case of the runs while you're trapped in a room the size of a closet that's bobbing up and down. I never thought Doc from "The Love Boat" was much of a physician and the clown you visit in the infirmary won't be either. At best he'll throw a couple of Imodium tablets at you and call it a day.

Misery loves company and when the virus hits a cruise ship, it spreads like wildfire. Probably a sizeable number of your "shitmates" will be sick at the same time. The virus can last 4-6 days which should more than cover your cruise time. If everyone on the ship gets the shits, you may be lucky enough to have raw sewage come down the walls of your cabin. It happened a few years ago when everyone on the ship became ill and the plumbing went out. Having the runs is one thing; shit running down your walls is another. Ahoy matey!!!!

Thanksgiving Night at a Walmart

I could never understand the logic behind late night shopping on Black Friday eve. After feasting all day on turkey and watching football you're going to leave your warm home after 10pm, drive to Walmart to do battle with trailer trash in hopes of getting a flat screen TV at a discount price?

This is yet another example of people's inability to just stay home. We don't live in the old USSR when people waited in line for days at a time for a roll of toilet paper. This is the United States of America and we are better than that. Our forefathers fought the redcoats, Nazis and communism so that we could enjoy football on Thanksgiving. For Christ sake, you can shop online without having to leave your house until you get the carpal tunnel syndrome. After spending a nice day with family you're going to risk your life for a fucking Christmas gift that your aunt will probably return anyway?

You can't blame Walmart and other retailers because they are in business to make money. Retailers have tapped into a moronic portion of society that's willing to leave their warm house on a holiday in hopes of getting something on the cheap. The only way I am leaving the house on Thanksgiving is if the house is on fire.

Why would I wait outside a store in the freezing cold with other pinheads like it's the Oklahoma land rush? Once those doors open, the crowd will push you into the store like sperm going up a fallopian tube. If you don't get crushed or trampled, are you willing to brawl over a limited edition Wii game while going through L-Tryptophan withdrawal? You have 365 days a year to shop for Christmas and I'm sure you can find better deals during that time than in one night in November.

Dive Bars

What can I say about a good old fashioned dive bar that has not already been said? Dive bars exist because the alcohol is cheap and attracts an unlimited amount of downtrodden barflies. Anything goes in a dive bar because the owners are never there and even if they are, they could give a shit about what goes on inside, and their patrons know it. Bad food, shitty service and terrible behavior by misanthropes would never be tolerated in an established bar or restaurant chain. Go jump on the bar at a TGI Friday and see what happens to you. If you do, get out of there as fast as possible because the cops are coming and you're going to be arrested. Do that in a dive bar and it probably wouldn't be noticed.

Wandering into a dive bar and not knowing the lay of the land can get you hurt very quickly. Drunkards resembling Star Wars creatures from the cantina bar scene will greet you with snarls through their missing teeth and will give you the hairy eyeball. They may not be blue or green but they're just as fucked up.

The eligible bachelors usually have dye jobs or bad toupees and prison ink tattoos. Burned out booze hound debutants squeeze their size fifteen asses into size five miniskirts and will blow smoke in your face. There's always someone selling coke or weed inside these places so you're lucky if they suspect you're a cop because they will leave you alone. You might catch a few dirty looks but you can live with that.

But if you are sized up as a stranger just passing through, you might get fucked with. Some dive bar inhabitants think of themselves as local warlords and do not appreciate strangers coming into their crib. They don't care that you just want to have a drink and spend money. Depending on the place and how much attention you bring to yourself, results may vary between getting shot to getting a pint glass smashed over your head.

I'm lucky to be alive because I've been in dive bars that Jon Taffer from "Bar Rescue" wouldn't have the balls to enter. Despite my stupidity I am here to talk about it. Even if you don't get messed with, do you really want to eat in a place that puts ice in the urinals?

Dive bars are not known for gluten free menus or healthy choices. Your head is going to ring like a church bell the following day from the flat tap beer you drank because they never clean the tap lines.

You're also going to have flames shooting out of your ass from the under cooked Hiroshima wings you had to have. Cheap booze and raunchy women are not worth risking your life or trying to save a few bucks. If you're going out for beer and wings, go to an established bar restaurant instead. Your stomach and your head will thank you for it.

Safaris in Faraway Lands

Here is another way to die a horrible death in a faraway land while dressed like an asshole at the same time. The preparation alone for a trip to Africa would be too much work for me. I hate to pack for a weekend getaway, I couldn't imagine the amount of crap I would have to take on a safari.

On top of that you have to get a ton of vaccinations and take horse sized malaria pills before you even get on a plane. I often struggle swallowing a multivitamin. Then you have to fly halfway around the world on God knows what airline to get to the Congo Republic. It's not like booking a trip to Vegas on Priceline.com where you can bundle a flight, hotel room, and rental car for a week. Maybe you can bundle a tent, canteen, and blowgun for a reasonable rate. I am pretty certain United Airlines doesn't fly nonstop to Botswana.

The closest I've been to a dangerous Safari was going to the now defunct Jungle Habitat in West Milford, New Jersey. It was one of the first attractions in the United States where you could drive dangerously close to jungle animals in your own car. It was managed poorly, causing several tragedies between man and beast which ultimately led to the park's closing after only four years.

My parents however thought it would be fun to experience a safari in neighboring New Jersey. My brother and I were crammed again into the back of my parents' 2 door Datsun B210 with no air conditioning. Being exposed to my father's chain smoking would now be considered child abuse, but there we were, navigating the park's roads in a smoke filled car.

It got so hot in there that my father was forced to crack open the window, just as a baboon jumped on the side view mirror. I watched in horror as the baboon got his hand in the open crack and fought my dad for control of the window as he was frantically trying to close it.

It was probably at about that time my father regretted not getting power windows. It was man versus beast alright, with my father crushing the little fucker's hand in the window. The baboon freed its hand and let out a blood curdling yell. The injured baboon called a 10-13 (officer needs assistance call) and other baboons descended out of nowhere and jumped all over our car. They shrieked and began to pound on the hood and roof of our little Japanese import.

Trapped in our hot car and surrounded by pink asses, we watched as one baboon grabbed the car antenna and bent it like it was a coat hanger. The park was packed and we were boxed in a line of cars with nowhere to go. My father slammed on the gas and pulled an evasive maneuver, going off road into a prohibited area while he swung the steering wheel from side to side. My brother and I looked out our back window in amazement, watching monkeys fly off our car like in The Wizard of Oz. The instigating baboon hung onto to the side view mirror like Indiana Jones, refusing to let go.

At about that time, we noticed we were being pursued by a safari vehicle yelling at us on a PA system, threatening to remove us from the park for my father's road rage. When our car finally came to a stop, the instigating baboon was still holding on to the side view mirror. He calmly sat up on the mirror and glared at my dad through the window. It became a Mexican standoff, with neither willing to concede. The baboon then grabbed his little dick, pointed it at the window, and pissed right at my father's face.

As the yellow stream sprayed his window, my father cursed the baboon but was powerless to do anything else. The baboon had won this round. He finished his piss and shook his dick to make sure he had gotten out the last drop. He then kind of smiled and vanished into the woods, probably off to tell his friends what he did to us. The 18 year old park ranger finally caught up to us and began to lecture my father who told him to save it and to lead us out of the park.

The moral of the story is that they are called wild animals for a reason. We should respect their privacy and admire them from afar and not go to New Jersey to see them.

There are two types of people who travel halfway around the world to go on a Safari. There are safari goers with guns, and safari goers with no guns. Both have too much money on their hands and not a lot of common sense. They're very different from each other, but both types travel to remote and dangerous locations to annoy or kill wild animals, all the while putting their own lives in danger. Let's examine the differences.

Unarmed Safari

Those who go on unarmed Safaris are self-proclaimed animal lovers. They want to get up close and personal with wild and exotic animals who could give a fuck that they traveled eight thousand miles to see them. They are greeted by exotic animals with the same reaction as an Alzheimer patient in a nursing home. Neither recognizes them, and both are unsure why they are being bothered.

They claim to love animals unconditionally, and they detest the circus and animal parks as exploitation and exhibitionism of wild animals. Of course they ignore the fact that for the most part, animals in captivity get 3 squares a day and premium medical care not available in the wild.

These self-proclaimed do-gooders never consider the fact that they are inconveniencing and stressing out the exotic wildlife they profess to love by stalking them in their own natural habitat. Don't you think gazelles have enough on their minds worrying about lions and hyenas without having a pack of jerkoffs dressed like a J. Peterman catalog follow them around, taking photos like the fucking paparazzi?

Naively, they put their lives in the hands of an unknown and underpaid guide who chauffeurs them around in a second hand open air jeep. The Serengeti, like the cross Bronx expressway, is not a place you want to have car trouble. If your safari vehicle breaks down, you're screwed. Imagine sitting in a disabled open air jeep, stuck on the plains. It's going to be hotter than balls when mosquitoes the size of birds start pecking at you. You wanted to see hyenas, well here's your chance because hyenas can smell the fear of a grown man shitting his pants from miles away.

You better hope your guide Mamadou has a rifle and enough bullets for Shezi and her friends. If you think your cell phone is going to work in the Dark Continent, guess again. I can't get a strong signal in Bradenton, Florida so good luck getting a bar out on the grasslands. Even if you do get your cell phone to work, who are you going to call, ghostbusters? Talk about roaming charges, the nearest cell tower is 300 miles away mounted atop a 5 foot hut. They don't have AAA in Africa so you better hope you're close enough to camp or that they have a second vehicle available to save your ass.

Those who go on safari without guns usually bring three to five thousand dollars' worth of camera equipment to preserve their experience in photos. Picture a middle aged pear shaped woman hanging from a safari vehicle, extending a half foot zoom lens to get a photograph of a resting lion. It is not a good idea. She probably looks like a marshmallow to the lion. When Mamadou steps on the gas unexpectedly, she's going to flop out of that jeep and become a s'more for the lion.

Is getting the perfect shot worth your life? You can watch the same shit on National Geographic, in high definition at home in air conditioned comfort. If you think your friends really want to see the stupid photos of your safari you're wrong. Oh sure, they will appease you and politely glance at your photos. But just like any stack of photos you're handed from a kid's birthday party, after the third one your eyes are glazed over and you're just going through the stack to get it over with.

Armed Safari

Those who go on a hunting safari are people of means. Let's be real, Taco Bell employees usually cannot afford a trip halfway around the world. Hunting deer and bear domestically doesn't do it for these people anymore. They feel compelled to raise the bar on their midlife crisis. Tired of the Corvette or of banging the secretary, they are looking for a new adrenaline rush.

Like a junkie chasing his first high, they are constantly looking for a new euphoric experience and will throw caution to the wind to get it. They'll spend tons of money shipping rifles and camera equipment through a multitude of countries. I had a crappy twenty dollar camera stolen from my luggage on a flight from LaGuardia to Tampa, can you imagine what must go on with baggage handlers at the airport in Papua, New Guinea?

Like their unarmed safari counterparts, they like to dress up as UPS drivers and sneak up on wildlife. Bu they have a different agenda. You see, they want to kill an exotic creature and then take a selfie standing next to it. After all the high fiving that ensues, they have Mamadou the tour guide decapitate the poor animal so they can have it stuffed and prominently displayed on their wall at home.

Can you imagine what it must cost to have an animal's head prepared for taxidermy and shipped back to the United States? You can buy the same animal's head at an estate sale back home for a hundred bucks. What are you going to do with the meat after you shoot one of these animals in Africa? It's not like Omaha Steaks that flash freezes their meat and ships it to your door. You're going to wait out in the African heat while Mamadou butchers your rhino for you?

My mother would yell at me if I made a stop with meat from the supermarket in the car, and you're going to trust rhino meat that's been out in the African sun for a few hours? Then you're going to trust the villagers to package the meat and ship it back to the United States? I would rather drink Mexican tap water than eat week old giraffe. About the same time you're convincing yourself that your wildebeest tastes like chicken, an undiscovered parasite is boring a hole into your colon and it's never going to leave.

Let's say you do get the meat home, who are you going to get to eat it with you? Your wife may put up with the lion's head in your den but she's not going to eat the paw. My hunter friends in New York were giving away deer meat towards the end of hunting season because everyone had had enough of it and you think your friends in your gated community are coming over for a beast feast?

Can you imagine getting the runs on safari? There are no port-a-potties or toilet paper on the African plains so you're going to have to take a shit in a bush where a cheetah may be taking a nap.

Those who go on armed safaris grew up reading and romanticizing about Ernest Hemingway and Teddy Roosevelt's exploits. Reading about something dangerous and stupid is one thing, acting on it is another. Granted, Teddy and Ernie had balls of steel traipsing around the world seeking conquest after conquest. Those were different times and there wasn't really much to do for fun back then. For all their courage and adventure, they lacked two basic amenities that would have changed the course of history if available back then, and might have eliminated their need to go on safari.

The invention of air conditioning and basic cable has made the need to dress up like an idiot and go on safari irrelevant. Do you really think a literary genius like Hemmingway would stop writing a novel in an air conditioned room with a view of the Florida Keys to run off to Africa and sweat his balls off? If Ernest had AC, he would have written more books than Danielle Steele. Between the AC and the mini bar they wouldn't have gotten Hemingway out of his room with a crowbar.

Teddy Roosevelt would have been hooked on National Geographic and Animal Planet like a heroin addict. Armed with high definition cable, he would have never had to adjust his monocle while critiquing "The Crocodile Hunter" reruns. Teddy would have had a blast running around in his boxers, liquored up and shooting at the flat screen in his suite at the Bellagio. Hey, what happens in Vegas stays in Vegas, right?

Let's say your hunting safari goes as planned. You get out of Africa alive and you killed a few exotic animals along the way. Everything went well and you're sitting on top of the world. You cannot wait to tell anyone who will listen about your conquests in the Dark Continent. As a matter of fact, why wait to tell them? You're social media savvy so you tweet and post photos of yourself standing next to your dead exotic carcass, just as the flight attendant threatens to throw you off the plane after telling you a third time to turn off your cell phone.

You're sitting up in first class, feeling like a million bucks, sipping your scotch and listening to Ted Nugent on your iPod, on your long flight back to the States. You da man, right?

Wrong! Bet you didn't think of the social ramifications, did you? Showing everybody how cock diesel you are by killing rare animals is not chic anymore. As a matter of fact it's worse than wearing fur, or even worse than wearing white after Labor Day. Society judges hunting differently these days and social media only exacerbates it. It's one thing to eat meat, but show folks the process of how it got to their plates and they look at it quite differently. If Roosevelt and Hemingway were alive today, posting photos of themselves on Facebook next to dead rhinos, PETA would have a bounty on their heads.

By the time your plane lands everyone in the western hemisphere has seen your photos. Some have very strong opinions about them and are voicing them quite loudly. Angry villagers in your subdivision are looking for you with pitchforks and torches and they aren't looking to come over to try your elephant burgers.

If you don't believe me, ask the dentist who made the mistake of killing a popular village lion in Africa. Once the story broke, he had to endure a global backlash for months. The expensive safari he took was worse for his dental practice than the invention of fluoride. The hunter became the hunted with protesters and camera crews camped out in front of his practice.

Traveling around the world to dangerous destinations for a photo shoot or to kill something makes no sense to me. Jet lag, disease, and trusting impoverished people with your life do not seem like a good time. If you really have to see wild animals up close and personal, there are plenty of places in the United States that are a lot safer. You can see the same animals at Lion Country Safari safely from the comfort of your air conditioned SUV.

If that doesn't do it for you and you still want to safely torment God's creatures while sweating your balls off, go to Gatorland in Kissimmee, Florida. There you can walk out on a pier that sits above a large moat filled with hundreds of alligators and crocodiles. For five bucks you can throw uncooked hot dogs at their heads, causing a feeding frenzy, while you're eaten alive by mosquitos and if you're lucky you may even contract West Nile or the zika virus!

Or you can visit your local zoo and safely watch nature's creatures blankly stare back at you through bars or plexi-glass like inmates on lockup. And just like in prison, the animals will sometimes throw feces.

When I was a small child, my mother took my brother Fredo and me to the zoo. My brother and I walked in front of the gorilla cage looking in awe at a large silverback who didn't appreciate two kids gawking and pointing at him. After a while I guess he had enough, and suddenly jumped up and picked up a pile of fresh shit and charged the bars. I ran to my right and Fredo being Fredo, did a 180 and ran back towards my mother. Mighty Joe Young nailed him in the back of the head with a hunk of gorilla shit. Did I ever mention how much I like gorillas?

In summary, stay away from places with large crowds especially at night or when people are drinking. If you like to travel, avoid going to places where diseases are rampant and medical treatment is scarce. There are so many things you can spend your money on besides a trip to a dangerous place that you may never come back from.

Chapter 9

It's Not Nice to Tempt Mother Nature

Man has been ignoring Mother Nature since the beginning of time and in turn she has been killing him just the same. Why do we foolishly believe we are above the elements? How many countless lives are lost every year due to the weather? Lightning, hurricanes, tornadoes… we all seem to think weather catastrophes are someone else's problem. If we took a little precaution and paid attention to the weather, we might just live a little longer.

Lightning

Of all the weather elements that can kill you, lightning gives you fair warning that it's headed your way. You'd have to be deaf not to hear the sonic boom of thunder that sounds like someone dropped a bowling ball on the floor. As the sky darkens, the wind kicks up and you feel a damp breeze. In the distance you can see magnificent flashes of light. The ballet of dancing lightning strikes is mesmerizing. Like laser Floyd without the music, you're hypnotized by lightning's beauty. Like a slow rumbling freight train blaring its horn through a small town, all the warning signs are there. For Christ sake, you can hear it coming.

But what do most of us do? Nothing, it's business as usual. We go on with our outdoor activities ignoring the fact that something very dangerous is going on right above us. The host at a barbecue assures his guests the storm is far away and there is nothing to worry about while he's flipping burgers over the five hundred pound metal grill. Emeril quotes some bullshit math/weather formula, inaccurately predicting how far the storm is by counting the seconds between flashes of lightning and the sound of thunder.

As the loud booms of thunder get closer, we continue to push our metal lawn mowers across our yards. The umpire hasn't called the softball game yet so it must be safe. Meanwhile lightning flashes high above as another middle aged man steps up to the plate with an aluminum bat in his hand.

"Caddy, hand me my 9 iron" is yelled by a drunken golfer on the 18th hole. Enjoying his fourth Arnold Palmer, he foolishly ignores his caddy's pleas to leave the green and head into the clubhouse until the storm passes.

"Nonsense, the last hole must be played", the red faced golfer says. Ignoring the lightning siren, he grabs his metal golf club at the mid-shaft and is bitch slapped by Mother Nature's lightning bolt. Hopefully he learns a valuable lesson, provided he lives.

Why is it that we lose our common sense during a lightning storm? We insist on going outside and grabbing an umbrella (or metal pole shrouded in vinyl) for protection. It's like putting on a bulletproof vest with no Kevlar panels; it's a false sense of security. The umbrella (or lightning rod) is then opened and pointed to the sky, daring Thor to strike us dead.

Why are we more afraid of getting wet than of getting hit by lightning?

Lightning has and will strike the same place twice, ask the Empire State Building or the Asian guy on YouTube who gets hit twice within three minutes. Standing under a tree isn't going to save you, and as a matter of fact it increases your chances of getting hit. The tree acts as a lightning rod and usually whatever is underneath it gets fried.

You're better off getting wet than electrocuted. Unless you're Roy Hobbs looking for a unique way to make a baseball bat, stay away from trees during a lightning storm. Another fallacy is that water attracts lightning, it doesn't, nor does it act as a shield. Staying in the pool is just as stupid as standing out in the open during a lightning storm.

A direct strike from lightning may not kill you, but you'll wish it did. Lightning follows the old adage, what goes in must go out. It won't hang around long but during the short time it's in you, it can cause a lot of damage. Lightning exiting your body is not pretty and can blow your hand, foot, toes, or genitals off as it says goodbye.

Roofers know how dangerous lightning can be. Watch a bunch of roofers when a lightning storm is approaching. The roof will resemble a disturbed anthill because they cannot get out of there fast enough. Between metal ladders and being thirty feet closer to Thor, they're not taking any chances with lightning.

To my knowledge there are only two people who had valid reasons to be out during a lightning storm. Both desperate men, Ben Franklin and Andy Dufresne had different reasons for ignoring common sense and tempting lightning's deadly power.

Serving a life sentence for a murder he did not commit, Andy Dufresne squeezed through the lower intestines of the Shawshank penitentiary sewer system and into a lightning storm, keeping one step ahead of Warden Norton and the sisters. After emerging from the sigmoid colon of the penitentiary, Andy tore off his shirt and ran for his life.

Oblivious to the lightning strikes high above, Andy could not care less.

He had bigger fish to fry, because if captured, Warden Norton would make good on his promise to cast Andy down with the sodomites. So for Andy, the light show above was like a Swedish massage compared to what awaited him if captured during his escape attempt.

Ben Franklin on the other hand was all about the science and was a colonial version of the Kardashians. A publicity hound, Ben was the Ron Popeil of his day. A walking infomercial, Ben would pitch his gadgets and ideas to anyone who would listen. His cheap inventions were inexpensive gag gifts for colonialists every Christmas season. Ahead of his time, he invented the odometer before the automobile and bifocals for people who couldn't read. Ben left many a colonialist scratching their powdered wigs with his inventions. If Ben were alive today, he would be working at Ye Ole Sharper Image kicking around a Hacky Sack and operating a remote control helicopter.

A jealous man, Ben always let his penis envy get the better of him. When his archrival George Washington had his portrait engraved on the one dollar bill, it didn't sit well with big Ben.

"Father of the country my arse" he said to himself. Ben became obsessed with getting his mug on the new hundred dollar bill that was about to be printed. If Ben could get his face on the hundred dollar bill, people would finally take him seriously. It would make him 99 times more valuable than his nemesis, Georgie. Ben correctly believed that having his face on the hundred dollar bill would achieve immortality. He needed a publicity stunt to set him apart from the other founding fathers that would secure his image in the wallets of Americans for decades to come.

Always curious about lighting and its power, he pondered if he could capture this spectacular energy despite the fact he didn't know what to do with it. Ben knew it could be dangerous but well worth the risk. After being told to "go fly a kite" by an angry shopkeeper who was tired of Ben's peddling of dollar store products, he decided to put the expression to use, literally.

Complicating matters was Ben's addiction to snuff (or colonialist cocaine). Not in the right frame of mind on that muggy afternoon in Philly, he armed himself with a kite, twine, and a stolen skeleton key courtesy of Ye Ole Motel Six and he put his plan in action.

Never fashion conscious, Ben looked the part of a "To Catch A Predator" scumbag in pantaloons and a long coat. A fat guy with a mullet and white powder under his nose running around the park with a kite is going to draw attention. Even in Ye Ole times Ben looked like a weirdo.

After running around for a while like an idiot, he finally got his kite high up into the stratosphere. Admiring his airborne contraption and enjoying his snuff, Ben got the shite scared out of him when a lightning bolt rocketed out of the sky and blasted Ben and his kite to smithereens.

Knocked on his arse, he didn't know what hit him. He rolled around on the ground for a while before getting up, singed and disoriented. He began yelling at the top of his lungs to the crowd that had gathered that he, Ben Franklin, had just discovered electricity despite the fact that nobody knew what the fuck he was talking about.

The lightning almost killed Ben and ruined his high but he had accomplished what he had set out to do. His publicity stunt gained him enough attention to secure his portrait on the hundred dollar bill. Although Ben Franklin never did capture lightning in a bottle, he was able to coin the phrase and acquire the trademark. At least that's how I imagine it anyway.

Ben wasn't the first or the last to get that warm and fuzzy feeling from lightning. All kidding aside, Ben Franklin was a genius who didn't know any better when he tempted lightning that day. You on the other hand, are not a genius, but you do have an advantage that Ben Franklin didn't. The Weather Channel makes going outside idiot proof.

Lightning is one of the easiest outside dangers to avoid. The best and simplest advice to survive a lightning strike is to stay away from it.

If you're outdoors when a thunderstorm comes around, go inside. There's nothing that important that cannot wait until the storm blows over. So go inside, grab a beer out of the fridge, and enjoy nature's light show.

Hurricanes and Tornadoes: Don't Say You Weren't Warned

Living in the United States, we have a much higher probability of surviving a hurricane than those living in third world countries. Advances in construction and building codes have made homes safer. As a kid, I remember taping Xs over our windows to prevent flying glass, or at least I think that's what we were trying to do back then.

Living in today's society with a 24 hour news cycle, there is absolutely no reason to be caught off guard by an incoming hurricane. Even if you only have basic cable, you can find a variety of news outlets like the Weather Channel to give you constant hurricane updates. Unless you live off the grid like the Unabomber, or don't have a TV, cell phone, or radio, you cannot say you weren't warned.

Hurricanes are like the Super Bowl for weathermen. Living in the shadows of the Ken and Barbie anchor team, they settle for the scraps. Being the caboose of the show, they are given 30 seconds to warn us about tomorrow's weather. With so much information and so little time, they are regularly crapped on for an incorrect forecast.

The weatherman is always the punchline of jokes or backhanded comments from the hip couple sporting the pompadour and bleached teeth. The only way to gain notoriety is to wear a stupid hat, hold a wild animal, or broadcast live from an air show. That is of course until a hurricane is on its way.

A weatherman is like an understudying for a famous actor during a Broadway play run. One day the famous actor has become ill and the understudy must stand in for him. His time has come and he cannot wait to get on stage. He's been creaming in his jeans his whole life for this moment. Right, wrong, or indifferent, he's going for it with both barrels.

Isn't it ironic that the weather man is finally getting his moment in the sun and it's at our expense because he's warning us about an imminent hurricane? It's show time and Chicken Little yells from the highest roof to lecture us about high pressure systems and show off fancy spaghetti plots. Armed with Doppler radar and satellite images in high definition, the weatherman warns of Armageddon and tells anyone who will listen to get out of Dodge. If you haven't gotten out in time, he warns you to hunker down which makes you feel like a wanted fugitive.

Procrastinating, you convince yourself that you have time to get out of town even if he's right about the storm. This is the same jerkoff who predicted a beautiful day last Friday when you took off from work to play golf and ended up getting soaked.

"Shame on me once", you say to yourself. But what if this idiot is right this time? Do I really want to roll the dice and get stranded without food and electricity for a week? You keep telling yourself that you have time and then you stop by the supermarket and all the bottled water and canned food is gone. You still think you have time when you stop by the hardware store and realize all the plywood, generators, and batteries are sold out. That's when it begins to dawn on you, "Maybe this Schmuck is right?" Like I said, you were warned.

Hurricanes can kill you in a variety of ways; Drowning, electrocution, disease, or being smashed by flying debris to name a few. Tornadoes spawned by hurricanes can uproot trees and toss them like toys on top of you.

For those of us living on the east coast, that alone greatly increases your chances of perishing during a hurricane. Man has always wanted a room with a view and has tempted fate by building homes too close to the ocean. Is the beautiful ocean view you have from your house built on stilts worth the danger of getting swept into the ocean during a hurricane?

More people die after a hurricane than during one. The fun begins when the weather clears and people come out of their mouse holes. If looting is your thing, you're in luck. You can loot 'til you drop during the days after a hurricane because police departments unfortunately will no longer shoot looters as they burn and pillage businesses. Maybe I am naive but why would you risk your life entering a structurally unsound building to steal a TV set? Never mind the fact you have no home to bring it to or electricity to power it.

I have never been one to pay much attention to anyone who is too passionate or hysterical about a particular subject. Weathermen are definitely frustrated thespians waiting for their chance on the big stage, or in their case, cable TV. I know they are a pain in the ass, preaching to us about how this could be the biggest storm of all time. And for the most part we take their predictions with a grain of salt. But what if they are right that one particular time we decided to ignore them? I would rather drive back into town safe and pissed that I listened to an idiot, than to get carried off by a twister or living in a homeless shelter dining on K rations provided by FEMA.

Tornadoes

Tornadoes, unlike hurricanes, usually won't give you much warning that they're coming. Tornadoes are like people who crash a party or never RSVP.

Growing up in the Bronx, we didn't have tornadoes but we did have crime to contend with, so I guess I was lucky in that respect. I saw a water spout recently that absolutely scared the living shit out of me. Having witnessed something that was so big and powerful shook me to my core.

I used to blow off tornado warnings when I first moved to Florida but after seeing a waterspout, I now take them very seriously. How many times have we seen trailer parks blown to smithereens? The images are frightening, like the guy with one tooth in his mouth explaining to a news crew how the tornado sounded like a freight train and how he survived by hiding in his prized chifferobe.

Storm chasers have to be out of their minds to follow tornados. I understand chasing a storm for science, in an attempt to understand how a storm operates and therefore coming up with ideas to survive and detect them. What I think is moronic is chasing a tornado just to post it on YouTube. If you and your Hyundai are carried off into the next county because you wanted to film a video, I'm sorry but you got what you deserved.

The national weather service now has the capability to warn when weather conditions are right for a tornado, even before they touch down. Cell phone carriers, cable companies, and radio stations interrupt our service with tornado warnings whether we want them to or not. The only way you wouldn't know if a tornado touched down near you these days is if you slept through one and you're probably better off if you did.

If a tornado touches down near you, go inside and hide in the frame of a doorway. Stay away from open doors and windows, and avoid green faced witches riding a bicycle.

Today most weather events are survivable if you pay attention to the news and are properly prepared. If you're homeless living on the street with no access to this book, you're shit out of luck. Even cavemen figured out they had better get their hairy asses into their cave to get away from the elements, so what's your excuse?

Chapter 10

You Couldn't Pay Me to Do That

Did you know the occupation you chose may impact how long you're going to live? Most of us spend eight hours, or a third of our day at work. Factor in the commuting and preparation for work, and you're lucky you have time to sleep.

Most of us have to work to pay our bills and to live a productive life. It would be nice if we enjoyed our jobs which would make getting through the day that much easier. But the reality is most of us don't like our jobs or occupations. We complain about the boss, company, or systems in place.

I enjoyed the vast majority of my career and never contemplated retirement until my last year. By then I had had enough and was running out the door like the place was on fire.

My dad was a butcher who worked long hours in terrible conditions. Being trapped in a meat freezer cutting slabs of beef with a band saw doesn't make for a glamorous life. He didn't enjoy his job but he had to do it. He had a family, mortgage, and financial obligations. He lacked the education to advance in the work force, so he did what he had to do to put food on the table. He wanted a better life for my brother and me, and he sometimes worked 7 days a week to put us through Catholic school where he thought we may receive a better education.

Our great nation was built by those willing to do the dirty work. Dangerous and unappealing work often goes unrecognized by those in the upper echelons of society. Bruce Springsteen dresses the part and sings about working class heroes while gouging his fans with high ticket prices and lecturing them about social responsibility.

Here is a look at those who do the dirty and dangerous work, often risking their lives to put food on their tables, while possibly shortening their lives at the same time.

Cops

"That job's dangerous, you know". My father stated the obvious when I told him I wanted to be a police officer. Since I was five years old, I had been telling my parents the same thing, but when I reached nineteen, it was dawning on them that I was finally serious about something.

Out of high school for a year and working menial jobs, my parents worried that my pipe dream of becoming a police officer would never pan out. I passed the police exam, went through the academy and went on to enjoy a twenty year career as a member of the New York City police department.

So how can I sit here and tell you not to take a job in law enforcement when I did it for over twenty years? Cops are near and dear to my heart and to this day, I would still assist a cop or law enforcement official who's fighting or chasing some scumbag, because at heart I still am a cop.

One night I was over my buddy's house while he was lecturing his ten year old son about doing his homework and the importance of receiving an education.

"Patrick, you can either grow old working at a desk or busting up your body, the choice is yours". My buddy then looked over at me and turned back to his son and said, "No disrespect to your uncle but if you don't mind being up at 3am getting shot at, you can go that route too".

I was a little taken back because I had never looked at my previous life that way. In that split second I realized my friend, who is an engineer, thought my prior career in law enforcement was dangerous.

I mean I knew it was dangerous but it never sunk in. It's kind of like reading the five page booklet you get at the pharmacy when you pick up your prescription. Your doctor prescribed the medication so you're not really going to read that pamphlet. You know there is some risk but you really don't want to know about it.

The public loves the police when they can solve their problems. Other than that, the public views cops as a pain in the ass. People don't like to be told what to do and who can blame them, I know I don't like it either. You only call the police when you have a problem, don't you? When was the last time you were planning a party and invited the police over?

As a society we walk a fine line with law enforcement. We need the police to keep us safe and protect us from those who prey on society. We give cops guns and the power to arrest and take away a person's freedom when they cross the line of the laws of the land.

The dark side of that is absolute power can absolutely corrupt. Sure, cops are drug tested, psychologically screened, and monitored for bad behavior. But sometimes a few bad apples get through giving fodder for charlatans to exploit a bad situation for their own selfish agenda.

Cops are under an unbelievable amount of stress because they are not allowed to have a bad day. Having a bad day in law enforcement can be deadly or get you on the six o'clock news for all wrong reasons. Most cops are more afraid of making the wrong decision and getting in trouble than getting killed, I know I was.

What most people don't realize is that cops wear many hats during the course of a shift and they're expected to be experts in every field. Psychologist, attorney, EMT, mediator, stuntman to cab driver, every split second decision they make will be scrutinized and second guessed if the shit hits the fan.

Cops are entrusted with a task that most would not sign up to do. They deal with predators who take what does not belong to them or with people who settle disputes with violence and sometimes with guns. Cops deal with every aspect of society and no one is exempt from calling the police. From the affluent to the homeless, anyone can be a victim on any given day. Attorneys, drunks, junkies, wife beaters, those who cannot take care of themselves, nobody is exempt from possibly needing a cop's assistance one day.

Constantly exposed to a revolving door criminal justice system that features a never ending cavalcade of human debris, cops become jaded and cold. They are expected to deal with criminals and the dregs of society who curse them, yet they are supposed to smile and treat them with respect. It takes its toll listening to people's problems day in and day out.

Settling a dispute between two parties while trying not to leave a bad taste in the loser's mouth is an impossible task. You're never going to please everybody because one party will feel you did not get their side of the story correctly. They may feel slighted and walk away hating you, provided they walk away and not try to do you harm.

Technology has leveled the playing field for law enforcement making it a little safer for those who serve. Form fitted bullet proof vests and guns with high capacity magazines have saved countless lives in law enforcement.

When I was hired in the eighties, I was given a 6 shot 38 caliber Smith & Wesson and was told how lucky I was that I had speed loaders. Can you imagine getting into a gunfight and running out of bullets after six shots? And that's not to mention trying to manually load bullets from your pocket or dump pouch while someone was shooting at you!

Believe it or not, cops are taught to shoot to stop an aggressor, not necessarily to kill. But shit happens when you challenge a cop with a weapon or engage in a dangerous activity that requires police attention and refuse to stop when ordered to do so. With that said, cops want to end their shifts and go home in one piece. So if you're looking to play games with someone who is better trained than you, you're usually not going to come out on top.

When I was hired, I was told the average cop's life expectancy was fifty five years old, or five years after retirement. A lot has changed after 29 years but cops still tend not to live as long as say librarians or college professors. If the bad guys don't kill you, your diet will.

Cops have the worst diet of any group of people who have ever walked the planet. If you're doing midnight shifts, you're eating dinner in the middle of the night and breakfast in the afternoon. Nothing's open but fast food places so you eat crap all week long. Pizza, burgers, or Jamaican beef patties, you're lucky you don't die of an intestinal blockage. Finding a roach coach in a shitty neighborhood is like hitting the lottery for a patrol cop. Drinking 5 cups of coffee to stay awake working a midnight is not going to increase your life expectancy. Cops are in Dunkin Donuts to stay awake, not to eat donuts you insensitive pricks.

Another downside to working in law enforcement is the prevalence of suicide. Working under constant and intense amounts of pressure, cops sometimes will crack. Cops are supposed to be superheroes, righting society's wrongs and keeping everyone safe. The reality is they are underappreciated and underpaid for what they are asked to do day in and day out. Constantly second guessed by the media, politicians, and society in general, it's no wonder why some feel misunderstood and betrayed and will take their own lives.

After years of putting on a facade of invulnerability they sometimes feel hopeless and weak. These are the very emotions they were not supposed to show or feel during their day job. Ironically they turn to their gun, a tool that kept them safe all those years, to take their own life.

It takes a certain type of person to become a police officer. You have to have a lot of common sense and not let things get to you. You have to be able to do things that are unpleasant and sometimes defy logic.

If you do decide to take a career as a police officer, I wish you well. My parting advice for anyone who takes a job in law enforcement and becomes seriously depressed is simple; if the job gets to be too much for you and you feel overwhelmed, simply resign and do something else. There is no shame in walking away from a career that you do not enjoy. In six months nobody will even remember you worked there anyway, there's no shame in it, believe me. Go do something you enjoy because life is too short.

Corrections Officers

Raised Catholic, I was taught about purgatory, a place between heaven and hell. Purgatory is kind of like a weighing station after you die. If you were a scumbag in life, you might have a surprise waiting for you at the pearly gates of heaven. Saint Peter may find you ineligible for heaven and send you to purgatory to reflect on your misgivings. It's kind of like going to summer school after failing a class. If you pass, you move on to your next semester which is heaven. If you fail to acknowledge you were a scumbag in your previous life, you get left back in hell.

I imagine purgatory to be like getting trapped in a hot elevator with a talkative person who has bad breath. It could be worse but you really want to get the hell out of there. If you are able to redeem yourself in purgatory, you may be able to take the elevator up to heaven and avoid the hot poker in your ass.

Choosing a career as a corrections officer puts you right in the middle of purgatory. You're not quite in hell because you get to go home every day, but you're as close to the devil as you have to be. You're not actually bunking in cells with inmates, but you are in their home for at least 8 hours a day.

While enjoying a carefree career as a correction officer, you are exposed to a whole host of diseases. Tuberculosis, hepatitis A through Z, and scabies are just some of the entrees on the menu. Most criminals blow off their annual doctor's visit and aren't in the best of health when sent off to prison. If you're a germaphobe or the guy who lines the toilet seat with paper before taking a crap, this may not be the occupation for you.

However if you always wanted to be a doctor and didn't bother to go to medical school, this may be right up your alley. One of your daily duties will be to conduct body cavity searches. Your day might start with looking up men's asses, searching for a shank or whatever contraband they may have packed in there. Think of it as a kind of perverse Easter egg hunt with grown men squatting naked and spreading their ass cheeks in front of you.

If there is an upside to working in a correctional facility, it's that you get to eat for free! Unless you brown bag it to work, you are eating what the inmates eat because there's no Jimmy John's down the street. You're locked in the penitentiary for the duration of your shift so you don't get to leave the grounds to grab lunch or a Starbucks coffee.

Guess who made that delicious meatloaf looking substance? That's right, the same guy doing 25 years to life who only last week you told to get off the phone. You think he remembers that interaction? You bet your ass he does because he has nothing but time on his hands. As a matter of fact, he has been motherfuckering you all week. That curly hair from his lower torso that just found its way into your meatloaf was no accident.

They say working 20 years in a correctional facility and factoring in overtime is equivalent to serving an eight year sentence. I had the luxury of dropping off criminals in jail, not babysitting them there. Getting shanked, shivved, or having feces thrown in my face is not my idea of a good time. You can't carry a gun in a correctional facility because you are outnumbered. In most correctional facilities you don't even carry a nightstick. It's you versus them, "mano a mano", so you better be in excellent shape or know how to make friends.

Sure you're in charge, but it's a facade. Inmates run the asylum and if you want to be a constant hard ass you're going to get jumped. Having visited correctional facilities many a time, I know they are quite noisy and you cannot hear yourself think. It's Bedlam in those places and the noise can be deafening.

Imagine being at a ten year old's birthday party with 100 of his closest friends who all curse. Everyone is screaming to be heard at the same time with no pauses or segues. It probably takes a correction officer at least an hour to clean all the shit out of his ears after every shift.

You're paid to guard terrible human beings who despise you with no scenic view, no music, or anything to take your mind off where you are. If you enjoy staring at teardrop tattoos all day long, you're in the right place.

If you really want to know what a correction officer has to deal with, watch MSNBC's "Lock Up". It runs continuously every weekend and will open your eyes to what goes on in our prison systems.

On the upside, the pay is good and comes with health benefits and paid vacation. In most cases after 20 years of service, you get to retire. But at what cost? The key to any benefits program is to be alive and well to enjoy them. I just wonder what is left of a person after a twenty year career as a correction officer.

EMTs

These poor guys are the Rodney Dangerfield of civil service. They don't make anywhere near as much as cops or firemen, nor do they have the power of arrest or carry guns, yet they are exposed to the same dangers and scumbags. The cops and firemen do seek them out though, because they have the secret cure to battle those weekend hangovers: pure oxygen.

Talk about no respect. Paramedics have to deal with the never ending ailing public that rarely if ever appreciates them. They are exposed to a variety of nasty bodily fluids that leak from every orifice. They work round the clock shifts in shitty neighborhoods, tending to one ailment after another.

Every paramedic I have ever met had a bad back from years of carrying junkies who overdosed or overweight slobs on gurneys who refuse to walk to the ambulance. I have seen paramedics raise the dead with a shot of Narcan or use a defibrillator to jump start a heart attack victim back to life.

Paramedics are spit on by drunks, stuck with hypodermic needles and called every name in the book by a thankless public. It's one continuous ambulance ride to the hospital after another as day turns to night and back to day.

Doctors talk down to them, and patients whose very lives they saved never take the time to seek them out to say thanks. There is no glory and certainly not enough money to deal with the dangerous and unappreciative public they deal with day in and out. I tip my hat to these guys because it takes a very special person to be an EMT or paramedic. And that type of person is definitely not me.

Linemen

This particular occupation combines two things that scare the shit out of me, heights and electricity. Any occupation that offers two ways to die is not for me. You either have to climb a pole or structure to get to a power line like a Flying Wallenda, or operate a bucket truck for your ascent into the sky. I would be praying to God that some idiot below didn't plow through the orange safety cones and slam his shitbanger into the back of my cherry picker truck, launching me from my bucket.

I am sure those guys know what they are doing but there is no room for error when you're working with electricity, especially high voltage. Get too close to a power line during an unexpected power surge and you will get fried like crisp bacon. Falling off a roof is bad enough, can you imagine falling off a high power tension line? Whoever finds your body will be amazed by your final ever advanced yoga pose that you managed to achieve on the concrete.

Maybe you don't mind heights or electricity and feel solace working up that high. That is of course until you are attacked by the symbol of freedom, the American bald eagle. She will inevitably claw the shit out of you for getting too close to her nest.

Commercial Fishermen

The History Channel devotes its programing to a host of shows demonstrating occupations you couldn't pay me to do. Commercial fishing, logging, or driving trucks on ice through Alaska, they seem to find people who have the balls to do things most of us wouldn't dream of.

Commercial fishermen are under a ton of pressure to come up with their quota of fish. They can only fish for certain species during certain seasons, and in the case of a fish like tuna, size does matter. They can be stopped and boarded at any time by the Jewish Navy who can inspect their ship and break their balls for a variety of reasons. They are out in all kinds of weather risking their lives to make a living within a small window of opportunity to do so.

In the case of the poor bastards who are commercial fishermen in Alaska, risking your life is all in a day's work. Unless I was on the run from the mafia or facing a long prison sentence, you wouldn't catch me anywhere near Alaska. The place seems like a good place to commit suicide. It's cold and always snowing and if that's not bad enough you sometimes get 24 hours of daylight. I can't sleep if there is a night light on, could you imagine trying to sleep through 24 hours of light? What does one do for fun in Alaska? Besides drinking and snowball fights, I cannot really think of anything.

Out on the cold and unforgiving sea, dressed like the Gorton's fisherman, you hope not to get thrown overboard by a rogue wave or crushed by a 500 pound crate of snow crabs you could just as easily buy at your local Piggly Wiggly. All the while you're getting yelled at by an unsympathetic bearded fat bastard who pilots your ship.

If you are unlucky enough to get launched overboard into the Bering Sea in the dark of night, it's over. That cute rain slicker you're wearing is going to fill with water fast and weigh you down like a marriage to a Kardashian. Both are unforgiving with the former killing you a lot quicker.

Even if you do survive your career as a commercial fisherman, your hands are going to look like the elephant man's from getting smashed by clanking metal pods. God forbid you get seasick; you'll be shit out of luck. The ship captain wouldn't return the boat to port if his own mother was onboard having an appendicitis attack. These are rough men whose lives and businesses depend on a small window of opportunity each season.

If you somehow become seriously injured on a commercial fishing boat, hopefully the captain calls the Jewish Navy to airlift you in a Moses basket to the hospital.

Half of the ship's crew is probably criminals on the run from somewhere. Why else would a guy from Florida travel to Alaska to fish? In Alaska you're not going to run into anybody who might recognize you and turn you in. It's not like being a fugitive and running into a guy you went to high school with 30 years ago at Disney World who saw you on "America's Most Wanted" and will drop a dime on you. There are probably 6 cops in Alaska, it's the perfect place to hide. So the question begs to be asked, you're going to trust some arch criminal with your life on the high seas for 30 days and 30 nights? Pass. No, thank you.

Plumbers

On face value this profession does not seem dangerous at all. I mean who has ever heard of the Roto-Rooter guy drowning in a toilet? When you think of a plumber, you think of a guy with his ass crack hanging out and his head buried under a kitchen sink. I have two friends who are plumbers and they say the same thing. Choosing a career in plumbing is a death sentence.

You're on your hands and knees all day long, trying to reach a pipe by fitting yourself in tight spaces like a contortionist.

A plumber's best friend has to be a chiropractor who works on backs that have the mileage of a professional twister player. But the most dangerous threat to plumbers is an invisible killer, germs. Shit, piss, vomit, you name it, it goes down your drains. At some point your toilet or sink is going to clog and inevitably you're in a world of shit.

I know a guy who almost lost his leg from a staph infection he contracted from a broken toilet. We have all tried to plunge a clogged toilet only making it worse and causing the toilet bowl levy to crest. This sends foul smelling water cascading to your bathroom floor and a visit from Mr. Hankey who mutates into multiple pieces.

You're over this shit so to speak, break down and call a plumber. At this point you don't care what it costs until of course the bill arrives. Four hours and 2 cans of air wick later, you're praying for the moment the plumber rings your doorbell. Plumbers are a lot like the police. You never think about them until you need them and then you cannot wait until they get there to save you.

Criminal

Ever wanted to be your own boss, make your own hours, work free of supervision and pay no taxes? Do you like to sleep in and are morally flexible? Well do I have a profession for you. It sounds like the perfect occupation or a work-from-home scam in Florida. But in reality there are a couple of million people out there involved in this line of work. The job is crime and those who employed by it are called criminals. I had a twenty year career trying to ruin theirs.

Academics and intellectuals will argue that most criminals were driven to a life of crime through social and economic conditions like poverty or a lack of opportunity. The "they don't any know better" excuse really does not fly with me. If you know right from left, then you should easily know right from wrong. Sure, people make mistakes and will do something stupid while drunk or in a moment of weakness.

I am not talking about them. I am talking about career criminals, recidivists or plain and simple scumbags. Those who from the time they get up in the afternoon, until they lay their head in the wee hours of the morning, are scamming and conniving to take what you own. They have no conscious and write off their dirty deeds as just the cost of doing business. Criminals are the epitome of those who take shortcuts in life.

There are plenty of downsides to being a criminal. You're going to have to look over your shoulder all the time because those pesky cops and federal agents are lying in wait for you to slip up. Technology has made it a little more difficult to be a criminal these days but that doesn't deter them one bit. DNA profiles, license plate readers, and face recognition software make crime fighting in the twenty first century sound like something out of the movie "'Total Recall". As a criminal if you think your only obstacle is law enforcement, you're wrong.

Sometimes victims will rise to the occasion and give a criminal a good old fashioned ass kicking or worse. If chicken soup is good for the soul then a dose of street justice will do wonders for a criminal's conscious.

I remember once up in The Bronx, a young woman came out of her building to meet her boyfriend who was waiting for her in his car parked around the corner. As she exited her building, she was greeted by a piece of shit, high on angel dust, who punched her in the face and knocked her to the ground. As she lay on the sidewalk, the scumbag took her purse and began to walk away. The girl began to get up and the scumbag turned around and punched her in the face again for good luck, knocking her down again.

Not waiting for a standing eight count, the brave girl got up again and ran in the opposite direction to her boyfriend's car. She and her boyfriend then pursued the mugger to a local park. The boyfriend, an avid weightlifter and bouncer, cornered the thief who made the mistake of picking up his hands to fight. Feeling strong from his first TKO, the mugger figured he would get another notch on his belt. Needless to say he had the angel dust knocked out of him by the young couple who used their fists and a 1980s anti-theft device known as "The club", which for all intents and purposes, was a club.

The only overhead a criminal has is incarceration. Criminals don't pay taxes so they really do not have a lot of write offs. Tools and materials to pull off their crimes are often stolen, so this career requires little startup capital. The only real and constant pain in the ass they have to contend with is the cops. Cops are bad for business.

If this little uplifting story has not deterred you from getting into a life of crime, let me tell you what happens to you after your initial arrest. Now keep in mind your experience is going to be different depending on where you get arrested. But I can give you an idea of what it's like to get pinched in NYC.

Let's say you always wanted to drive a Mercedes Benz but never got around to getting a job or saving enough money to purchase one. Getting up at 11am, smoking weed and spending most of your day playing video games does not make for an impressive resume. Anyway, you're walking by a full service carwash and notice an S-class coming out of the dry cycle. The four foot tall guy who makes three dollars an hour drying off cars walks away to grab a Shammy. That's when you decide it's miller time. You jump in the driver's seat of the Mercedes and lo and behold, they were nice enough to leave the key in the ignition for you.

You didn't want to hold up the line so you punch it. Sliding out of the car wash sideways and dragging a bunch of South American migrant workers along, you exit in style. You blow a couple of lights to make sure you put a little distance between you and your competition, just to play it safe. What's a couple of red light tickets compared to grand larceny auto? You get the Benz to your block and you da man as you show it off to your boys and the bitches. The only problem is you stole a loaded Benz that comes equipped with Lojack, GPS, and sonar. Within an hour you and your Benz are tracked down.

You get boxed in traffic by ten men in blue, each pointing guns at you while introducing your face to the cold pavement. You're handcuffed, hands behind you, and shoved into the back of a police car to be transported to a local police station. The back seat will smell like piss because the last occupant that sat back there was nice enough to empty his bladder for you.

Inside the police station, the arresting officers take you over to the front desk and take everything out of your pockets. Your belt and shoelaces are removed because they don't want you leaving early and you might consider using those to hang yourself. You're fingerprinted and photographed and your arresting officer will prepare the appropriate paperwork.

You are placed in a large cell with other scumbags who are either sitting or sleeping on a concrete bench or floor. You're going to be there anywhere from two to six hours, so get comfy. If you're lucky enough to get arrested in a slow precinct, you may have the cell all to yourself. If you're arrested in a busy precinct, you might be standing up surrounded by thirty criminals who may want your new sneakers.

If you are offended easily by others' lack of personal hygiene, you're in the wrong profession. Precinct holding cells stink because the homeless and criminals tend to not bathe as often as most of us. The homeless also tend to not have the healthiest of diets and suffer from gastrointestinal disorders that can result in some pungent, ripe farts.

After a couple of hours, your arresting officer will take you out of your cell and you're handcuffed again, placed in the back of another pee mobile, and transported to the dreaded central booking.

All five boroughs of New York City have a central booking facility. Some are better than others but believe me, they all are terrible. It's always crowded inside central booking and sometimes you will have to wait outside for an hour, with other handcuffed prisoners and cops on a line that goes around the corner.

Once inside, your cuffs will be removed and you will walk through a magnetometer. You will be searched again and placed in what's called the bullpen. The bullpen is a very large cell used to accommodate a large volume of prisoners. The bullpen in central booking makes a holding cell in a police precinct look like the Four Seasons hotel in Vegas.

If you thought it was crowded in the precinct holding cell, this place is pandemonium. Think of central booking as a catch basin that filters every arrest from each borough. Just to give you an idea of how busy central booking is, Brooklyn has 23 police stations and every arrest must go through processing at central booking at some point of the day.

If you're a picky eater, you're shit out of luck. You might get a baloney and cheese sandwich and a cold cup of coffee, depending on how long you're in there. Sometimes it can take up to 3 days before you see a judge, so sit tight. When you finally *do* see a judge, your bail will be set, depending on your criminal record or how the judge feels that day. If you cannot make bail, you will be sent to Rikers Island until your case is resolved.

If you are sentenced to state prison time, you get an all-expenses paid bus ride to a correctional facility in upstate New York. There you are thrown into gladiator school with guys a lot tougher than you. Some of your new roommates have nothing to lose because they are serving life sentences. Pissing off a guy already serving life may mean losing yours.

After they find your body in your cell, an investigation will begin. Your roommate will be given another life sentence, hey, what's one more, and your family will be notified of your death. If your family does not claim your body, you will be buried on the prison grounds cemetery in an unmarked grave. Your department of corrections number stamped on a small wooden cross will be the only indication of your existence.

If on the other hand, you decide to play nice with your new roommates, you're going to have to join a gang or be victimized by bigger and tougher inmates. Everything from phone use, cigarettes, and food portions will be taxed by bullying inmates who continue to prey on others despite the fact they are in prison for the very same behavior.

If you have ever been appalled by the conditions of a public restroom, wait until you see the amenities in "the can". It's not Christian bible camp, and for the most part everyone in prison is of low moral character so anything goes. Disease and rape, yes rape, are just a couple of the things you have to look forward to during your time in a correctional facility.

No matter how bad you think your life is, it can be a lot worse if you choose a career in crime. No amount of money is worth losing your freedom over. If you don't mind sharing a bathroom with 3,000 people, or looking over your shoulder every day to stay alive, then by all means break most of the Ten Commandments and see where it gets you.

Unless you're retired, disabled, on welfare, or a trust fund baby, we all have to work. There are plenty of career paths you can take without risking or shortening your life. You only get one chance on this earth so you may as well be happy and safe and earn an honest living as you play the game of life.

Chapter 11

Never Confuse Balls with Stupidity

During a family vacation in Florida, my brother argued with my father about going parasailing. Dad was well aware of my teenage brother's ability to hurt himself and would not let it happen. Fredo demanded to know why my father wouldn't allow him to break his pelvis. My father, who had a low tolerance for stupidity, took a puff from his Lucky Strike and spoke these words of wisdom.

"Never confuse balls with stupidity, there's nothing to be gained here, except a hospital visit".

If my brother injured himself parasailing, my family would have been screwed. What was the upside here? A hospital visit, medical bills and being stranded in Florida for an indefinite period of time? My father was right, why would you do something dangerous for no other reason than self-gratification?

Having balls is one thing, stupidity is another. My father tried to explain the difference to my brother countless times. But Fredo being Fredo never heeded my father's advice and continues to get the two confused to this day, engaging in activities that are hazardous to his health. Like I said earlier, you cannot save someone from themselves.

Being the polar opposite of my brother, I could never understand why someone would risk their life for an adrenaline rush. Be it for convenience, pleasure or just because you can (dog licking his balls again), dangerous activities can leave you with pins in your back, eating through a straw or a lot worse. I was never a daredevil like my brother and always had the thought of injury in the back of my mind so I never attempted half the shit he did.

We've all fantasized about doing something fun and dangerous. Most of the time our common sense will kick in, saving us from doing something that would have gotten us killed or seriously injured. I myself have always wanted to smash someone over the head with a guitar. It's not going to happen because I don't live my life as a professional wrestler, I don't have a guitar, and I don't want to get arrested. You only get one life, so why would you risk death or having one leg shorter than the other for no logical reason?

Young people get balls and stupidity confused the most, although there are those who never mature and continue to thrill seek well into their golden years. Some of these dangerous activities are expensive and require the participant to have the means to afford them. Who would have ever thought it would be expensive to get yourself killed?

Those Magnificent Men in Their Flying Machines (who sometimes crash their planes into a golf course)

I'm sure that in 1903, in Kitty Hawk, North Carolina, there were more than a few people in the crowd saying "Those two dickhead Wright brothers are going to get themselves killed" as they gathered around to watch the Wright brothers attempt the impossible. There wasn't a lot going on entertainment-wise in those days so if 2 idiots wanted to kill themselves in spectacular fashion, everyone came from miles around to see it.

Thank goodness Orville and Wilbur Wright ignored the naysayers and went on with their plan to build and fly the first airplane. I'm guessing with names like Orville and Wilbur, they were used to getting their balls busted and ignored what people said or thought about them anyway.

Often mistaken for the Smith brothers cough drop duo, these aeronautic pioneers set out to make their mark in aviation. What they were attempting at the time seemed idiotic to conventional thinking. They proved everyone wrong and other geniuses went on to perfect flying, making it the safest form of travel. The Wright brothers definitely had balls. Now here's a look at the stupidity.

I myself do not like to fly and find it a necessary evil. If you have to travel over 500 miles and don't have a lot of time on your hands, you fly. Today thousands of commercial flights take off and land every day all over the world without a hitch. You may get bumped or delayed and receive shitty service. You may have to sit next to some fat bastard who rubs his sweaty body up against you while you inhale recycled farts circulating around the cabin.

But look on the bright side, your flight attendant may be hot and you will arrive alive! I am not saying the airline industry does not deserve criticism for their delays and imaginative ways to nickel and dime the consumer to death. But what we take for granted in flying commercial airlines is the safety factor. A lot has changed since that day in Kitty Hawk, but I think a lot of us have lost sight of how safe we are when taking a commercial flight.

When flying a commercial airline in the United States, you're getting 2 professionally trained pilots who are regularly drug tested and held to the highest standards. There is also a very good chance that at least one or both of your pilots have military flight training, making them the best trained in the world. Commercial pilots must attend annual certification retraining in flight simulators and practice different techniques to employ in the case of an emergency.

Commercial airplanes are checked after every flight and serviced at regular intervals. Maintenance records are required and examined regularly by the FAA. If the pilot so much as feels the plane is not running correctly, the flight is delayed or canceled while the plane is serviced.

If you fly a commercial airline, your chances of perishing in a plane crash are infinitesimal. In the rare instance a commercial airplane does crash, the news outlets will cover it to death. In the era of the 24 hour news cycle, you cannot avoid hearing about a commercial airline crash for weeks after it happens. Greta Van Susteren will interview everyone from the victims' families to the guy who stocked the flight with toilet paper. Geraldo, being the vulture he is, will be at the crash site 15 minutes before even first responders arrive, carrying on like it's the second coming of the Hindenburg.

I agree that a plane crash is a big story and should be covered, but come on, the news outlets overdo it. Here is an interesting fact, the odds of dying in a commercial airplane pales in comparison to those who fly their own private planes.

On the other side of the coin, when a private plane crashes you'll never hear about it unless it's local and even then it will only get very minimal coverage. No Greta or other dishonest self-promoting clowns will be on it because that's beneath them and it's not worth the time they would have to spend in the makeup chair.

News outlets love a big splash and would rather cover a commercial airline crash that kills over a hundred people versus a small private plane crash that kills two. If they are sending a news truck over, they want to see blood. The truth is more private planes crash than commercial airliners though we seldom ever hear about it.

So the question begs to be asked, If you have to fly somewhere and can get William Shatner and his friends at Priceline.com to get you a good deal on a commercial flight, why would you pilot a small puddle jumper yourself?

Of course the answer is because they can, which goes against my father's good advice. When I get on a plane, it's going to have a toilet, a flight attendant, and I'm flying to a destination with a purpose. I know what the sky looks like so there's no reason to fly a small propeller plane just for shits and giggles or to marvel at the clouds. I know from watching the History Channel that propeller planes worked great during WW2, but why would you risk your life with old outdated technology today?

I know a few people who own and fly their own planes and they've been nice enough to offer to take me flying, and I always refuse.

I'm not placing my life in the hands of a well to do retired civil engineer going through a midlife crisis who decided to buy a new toy. Would you trust your life to an amateur doctor? The key word here is amateur.

Amateur pilots don't fly every day nor are their planes maintained as well as a commercial plane. Have you ever driven past a small airfield? They look like fenced in abandoned golf courses. Do you really think the Dr. James Andrews of airplane mechanics works on planes at a small airfield? I'm not trusting Lowell from "Wings" with my life.

I'm going out on a limb here and will guess that the guy manning the flight tower at a small airfield, if there even is one, is not in the same league as an air traffic controller at a major airport. Did you know most small airfields don't even have an air traffic controller?! A first come, first served method of taking off and landing at an airfield does not sound safe to me. Nor do I think a windsock is a substitute for professional weather equipment. If you want a comparison of what it's like to use inferior technology, the next time you get lost try roughing it with a compass or the sun instead of your GPS and see how far you get, provided you ever get anywhere.

So why on earth would you trust a guy with a very dangerous hobby to take you for a ride in the clouds? I've lived a very exciting life as a NYPD cop, complete with car and foot chases. I don't have to sit next to the Great Waldo Pepper telling me we have to attempt an emergency landing on the fairway of some golf course for me to feel alive.

The overhead of owning your own plane is very costly. The plane itself is big bucks and I'm sure the fuel is expensive as well. I shit bricks when the price of gas goes up a nickel at my 7-11. If you own a plane, you're probably not really worried about fuel cost but it still factors into the equation. It's not cheap to fly your own plane, it's all about the convenience.

If you have this kind of money, you most certainly can afford to fly first class commercial to anywhere in the world. I'm not against someone who has the means to own or fly their own plane, I'm just not the guy who is going to go up into the sky with you.

Harrison Ford once said he sometimes jumps into his airplane just to fly up the coast of California for a cheeseburger. So what happened to Indiana Jones last year? That cheeseburger almost cost him his life when he crashed his vintage WW2 plane into a golf course in California. This is the same guy who stapled a hat to his head so it wouldn't fly off when he rode a horse in Raiders of the Lost Ark.

You would think he had enough excitement in his life. I have nothing against Indiana Jones, but why wouldn't a guy with that kind of money and who is married to Calista Flockhart find something safer to do? There are plenty of other things you can do to remind yourself that you are alive.

You're either a professional pilot or an amateur so stick to what you know and you will live longer. The difference between being an amateur versus a professional can be best summed up by a story a friend told me when he was a doorman over thirty years ago in New York City.

Late one night, Art Garfunkel and the great Jack Nicholson came into my buddy's building after a night out and asked him to take them up in the elevator. My star struck friend obliged and the three entered the elevator. On the way up, Garfunkel began complaining to Nicholson that Hollywood was not taking him seriously as he tried breaking into acting.

Nicholson looked through his signature dark shades, cocked his head and began playing air guitar. "Artie, you're a rock and roller, not an actor" he said in his raspy voice.

My buddy almost burst out laughing as Jack went on to say, "Artie, you made it in life, be happy playing your guitar".

I'm guessing Jersey Jack couldn't understand why a music icon like Art Garfunkel would risk tarnishing his legendary status as a musician by failing as an actor.

My point with this long winded anecdote is if you have the money to buy a plane, have a professional fly it for you because unlike Art Garfunkel's failure as an actor, your failure as a pilot will cost you your life. You want to fly, fly commercial you'll live longer and hopefully you'll get free peanuts.

Motorcycles

I've never ridden a motorcycle but I can ride a bicycle and drive a stick shift, so I'm guessing if I really wanted to ride a motorcycle I could. I just never saw any point in it. Motorcycles remind me of a bottle rocket without the stick. Riding one seems to just be searching for an accident. You can be the safest driver in the world but if somebody taps you while you're riding a motorcycle, you're fucked.

A friend once told me there is nothing like the feeling of having the wind blow in your face and hair while riding a motorcycle. So sex, having a child, or buying your first home isn't as exciting? You want the wind blowing in your face, go buy a fan because it's a lot cheaper than the prosthetic leg or motorized wheelchair you're going to need after your accident.

During my first trip to the DMV after I moved to Florida, they were giving out bumper stickers that read "Look twice - Save a life, "motorcycles are everywhere". I thought to myself, I know how to drive a car safely but accidents do happen. Why should I take extra precautions for someone who is doing something dangerous around me?

When you're driving a car, you are encased in a metal box with seat belts and protective airbags that will go off in your face in the event of an accident, whether you want them to or not. If you talk on your phone without a handless device, or text while driving, you will get pulled over and get a summons stuck in your ass. Operating a motor vehicle in most states requires wearing your seatbelt. Recent traffic and safety regulations were put on the books because Insurance companies got tired of paying out claims. They lobbied the government to pass and enforce more traffic regulations.

But I'm supposed to be on the lookout for a helmetless, shirtless guy in shorts and flip flops riding a motorcycle, begging to get himself killed? Did you know some states allow you to ride a motorcycle without a helmet, provided you pay for extra coverage on your motorcycle's insurance policy? Like I said, I'm not big on telling someone what they can or cannot do, but let's get real here. I have to wear a seatbelt and not use my phone while driving a mailbox, but someone whose body is totally exposed, with no protection, riding a rice rocket a foot off the ground has the option to not wear a helmet? What am I missing here? That helmet you should be wearing might keep you alive but it might not keep you from being a quadriplegic.

If you're wearing a helmet not approved by the federal Department of Transportation, you're significantly increasing your odds of brain injury. An Illegal helmet that looks like the Nazi helmets will not fool the cops who pull you over, nor will it save your life. It only covers about two thirds of your head and has no face shield that would have kept the bugs from flying into your eyes and pebbles from chipping your teeth.

If you do chose to play it safe and wear an authorized helmet you will look like the "Great Gazoo", but it will increase your chances of surviving a motorcycle accident. You might look like you're ready for a walk on the moon, but your chances of survival are better.

Now if you want to be a total rebel and go helmetless, your chances of surviving a motorcycle accident are not good at all. The risk of brain damage or severe disfigurement jumps significantly higher. Gary Busey wasn't wearing a helmet when he smashed his head into the curb during his accident and he's fine, right? Who needs that stupid looking helmet that will mess up your hair? Can you imagine what your hairline will look like after they put a metal plate in your head?

Proper riding gear like jeans, boots, and a leather jacket can also significantly reduce your injuries if you take a spill on your motorcycle. If you want to look cool wearing only a pair of shorts and a thin tank top while riding, you're begging for a skin graft because the sidewalk will peel your skin off like a cheese grater.

Say you do everything right and wear the proper helmet, clothing, and don't weave in and out of lanes like a dickhead begging for someone to hit you. Through no fault of your own, you get hit by another vehicle or just go down on your motorcycle. You're now a Raggedy Ann doll at the mercy of whatever just hit you. If you're lucky you may only get road rash but that's not guaranteed. The sad reality is you might wind up losing a leg, but on the bright side you may get a role as Captain Jack Sparrow's lackey or you could end up with a motorized wheelchair which you operate by blowing through a tube.

When I was a cop I handled numerous vehicle accidents and those who got it the worst were riding motorcycles. I was called to a motorcycle crash in a gym parking lot in The Bronx one summer evening. When I arrived, there was a new high performance Honda motorcycle laying on the blacktop, next to a young teenager whose head looked like a smashed melon. He was lying motionless next to the brick wall of the building he crashed against.

He and his buddy had stolen the motorcycle and were performing stunts in the empty parking lot on a Sunday afternoon. The problem was the kid underestimated the power of the motorcycle and smashed head first into the brick wall with no helmet. His head actually pushed the bricks back a few inches into the rear of a store.

An old timer drove up to see what was going on and said to me, "Too bad he wasn't going 10 mph faster, he would have made it inside the store and you could have charged him with burglary".

I have friends who ride motorcycles and it's their right to do so. I'm not lobbying to take away anyone's rights here, I'm simply saying if you want to live longer, this is yet another avoidable activity that will put you in harm's way, plain and simple.

A few years ago my brother Fredo had asked me if I knew when the next police vehicle auction would be held. I asked why and he told me he wanted to buy a used motorcycle to commute to work. I told him I didn't know when it would be, and even if I did, I wouldn't give him the information.

The NYPD has seized motorcycles and cars that sit out in the weather for months or years at a time until they are auctioned off. It's also been my experience that people who lose their property to the police usually didn't take care of it very well in the first place. On top of that, Fredo is married with children, so why on earth would he put his health on the line to save 40 bucks a month on gasoline?

He was perplexed and demanded to know why I was being a dickhead like our father who wouldn't let him go parasailing as a teen.

"Fredo, I'm not going to help you lose a leg" I told him, "It's bad enough that you're going to end up in a wheelchair, I don't want to be the one to have to listen to mom and dad blame me for it". He argued the point a while longer until I hung up on him. Like I said, I call him Fredo for a reason.

Super Cyclist

Cyclists are another group of dickheads who defy logic by putting themselves in harm's way while attempting to look chic at the same time. Cyclists falsely believe "I spend a lot of money on my hobby therefore I am invincible". If you Wikipedia cycling, they credit the so called sport for saving the planet by cutting down on fossil fuels by using clean energy.

Wikipedia also goes on to say cycling reduces noise pollution, traffic congestion, parking problems, and varicose veins. I will concede on the parking but have you ever been unlucky enough to end up behind a pack of these assholes when you're driving your car? Talk about traffic congestion. Traffic slows to a snail's pace because everyone is terrified to pass the flock since they insist on riding right on the outside line of the bike lane. God forbid you hit a cyclist with your car, talk about noise pollution.

I'm guessing the Wikipedia author for the cycling entry has a Lance Armstrong poster on his wall and bikes to work every day, saving us from those terrible fossil fuels. The only problem with Wikipedia's definition is that cycling is an arbitrary task performed by those who have money to spend on a lifestyle. You cannot be a cyclist without the ensemble and all the high tech gear that goes with it. I'm pretty sure Wikipedia's definition isn't talking about the folks who cannot afford a car and use a bike to get around. Great, you're saving the planet by cycling but how much can you bring back from the store on your bike? Picking up your kids from school? Forget it.

Cycling is an activity that usually includes other cult followers although it can be performed alone. We've all seen them on weekends peacocking on our roads and begging for attention. They like to travel in packs and wear bird shaped helmets that make them look like a flock of pigeons released from their coop to get their weekly exercise.

Speaking of pigeons, the bike lanes they are supposed to ride in are about the width of a ledge only a pigeon could occupy, yet the cyclists insist on riding two abreast, daring motorists to pass them.

Like lemmings, they will follow the leader of the pack blindly, sometimes to their own peril. If the fool leading the pack makes a bad decision or suddenly stops short, the rest of the conga line goes down like dominoes. If you're unlucky enough to hit one of them with your car, you will pay through the nose whether it's your fault or not.

You're always going to be in the wrong if you hit one of these schmucks with your car. A guy moaning in a hospital bed with an IV drip or catheter in his dick is going to be in the right regardless of what idiotic thing he did to get himself there. On top of that, he is going to get some form of financial settlement because it's just the way of the world these days. Unfortunately the cop taking the accident report is not going to be sympathetic to the scratches or dents on your hood when there's a twisted bicycle and an idiot rolling around on the ground.

They squeeze themselves into skin tight spandex suits that accentuate every pubic hair and convince themselves that these getups make them aerodynamically superior. In reality they look like brightly colored bratwursts.

Making sure your bike matches your ensemble and accessories is key, or you will be looked down upon by the color blind pack you roll with. Leaving the house for a ride with a mismatched water bottle and helmet is a cyclist faux pas and should be avoided at all costs.

In addition to color coordinated water bottles, air pumps, etc., the ultimate toy in the cyclist world is a double bike rack that mounts to the top of your vehicle. I sometimes fantasize about one of them driving through a low clearance garage, shearing off a three thousand dollar bicycle mounted to the roof of a Volvo.

Gliding at high speeds on a sliver of road, they sit high atop their cycles made from some lightweight aluminum alloy carbon fiber metal found only on Krypton. With their asses suspended high atop their bike seats, hemorrhoids are a distinct possibility. I often wonder if anyone has ever sat down the wrong way while wearing one of those tight lycra outfit and pinched off a testicle?

Anytime I see a pack of them parading around in their costumes, I'm reminded of my youth and the Marvel or DC comic books I used to read. Each dressed slightly different but the same, like superheroes in brilliantly color coordinated outfits. Do they honestly believe putting on a ridiculous riding costume makes them invincible to all the dangers of the outside world?

Cyclists suffer from a condition known as "huevos grandes" when riding in large groups and exhibiting a pack mentality. It enables a cyclist to safely yell expletives like a barking Chihuahua at pedestrians or motorists whom they perceive have not given them proper road respect. Instead of safely riding in a park, they foolishly insist on inserting themselves into vehicle traffic, believing the bike lane is a safe haven from all the evils of the outside world.

Superheroes Are Invincible, Cyclists Are Not

Superheroes have super powers which give them the ability to do some pretty cool things. Cyclists have super egos which enable a false sense of security and lead them to believe they have the right of way on all roads.

Superheroes have protective armor which makes them invincible from injury. Cyclists wear Styrofoam Coleman coolers on their heads, so they can have an open casket at their funeral.

Superheroes have super hearing and vision which enables them to see through walls and hear sounds miles away. Cyclists have a postage stamp size mirror mounted on the side of their cooler, giving them zero visibility.

Superheroes have a sixth sense to avoid danger. Cyclists have screws and pins in their backs. Cyclists really should go find a park for everyone's sake.

Superheroes can fly through the air and can travel to the outer universe. Cyclists can only become airborne after being hit by a car, then they ride in an ambulance.

Superheroes have a fortress of solitude where they can recharge their super powers. Cyclists ride to Whole Foods in search of a $3 bottle of water.

Superheroes hang around with other superheroes and fight evil. Cyclists look up to Lance Armstrong and his missing testicle.

Then you have the lower tier bicycle riders who are looked down upon by super cyclists. These are the un-scrubbed rubes who do not wear color coordinated outfits. They refuse to buy the proper gear or accessories. The 1980s fanny pack that holds their keys and wallet will do just fine. These folks are going to get hurt as well, they just aren't going to spend the money to do it.

They're not fashion or trend conscious so they won't spend the cash on a newfangled bicycle or spandex outfit because they couldn't care less how they look. The last time they bought a new bicycle was in 1982. They will either pick up a bicycle at a garage sale or buy the Walmart $49.00 special. Never bothering to check the tire pressure, oil the chain, or adjust the brakes, they simply jump on the bike and away they go.

The only helmet these guys have is a hockey helmet hanging in the garage. Hey, it's better than nothing, right?

Unlike the super cyclists, these guys know their place in society. They ride a lot slower and safer and usually only pose a serious risk of injury to themselves and not to others. They never ride in the street and tend to stick to the sidewalks or public parks.

Their riding attire is the polar opposite to the super cyclist color coordinated outfits. Their ensemble is jeans, baggy sweat pants, and sneakers that cost under ten dollars and offer no arch support.

They tend to be overweight with little to no coordination. They are heart attacks waiting to happen and after about two blocks on the bike, begin to sweat profusely. Sometimes they will remove their sweater and wrap it around their waist. After another two blocks, the sweater will loosen and jam the front brakes or chain below, resulting in a head first pirouette over the bicycle that would make Dorothy Hamill jealous. If they survive the crash, they often require extreme dental work to fix their newly acquired jack o' lantern smile.

The people I really cannot understand are the morons who put their dog or cat in a basket mounted to the front of a bicycle. Launching your pet from your bike isn't going to end well for them. If you really don't give a shit about yourself that's one thing, but if you love your pet, why would you put its life at risk? The poor dog sitting in the basket mounted to the front of the bike does not know any better, but the jerkoff doing the peddling should.

Then you have the idiots who think they are in Thailand and tow a pet rickshaw behind them. What these mamalukes don't realize is that when they tip over, so does the rickshaw, crushing the dog. Why don't you just take the dog out for a walk? Whose idea was it to have humans chauffeuring pets on a bike?

I could get more into people putting their pets in harm's way, but that's for another book.

A Three Hour Tour

Boating or sailing is another fun way to die, if you don't know what you're doing. What could be nicer than going out on a boat to enjoy the sun and do a little fishing? Boating is another expensive hobby in which you can lose your life very quickly if you don't plan for the unexpected, or are inexperienced.

The best thing about boating is that you don't need a license to get yourself killed. This has always fascinated me because you can get yourself or others killed just as easily as driving a car or plane without any formal training. You're operating a vessel that is powered by a motor or wind propulsion and you don't need a license? But with like a plane or car, you are not allowed to operate a boat while inebriated because the same rules apply for drinking and driving on the high seas as on the road or skies.

Your boat can be stopped and boarded indiscriminately by the Jewish Navy or local marine patrol who can demand to inspect your equipment or lack of thereof. Law enforcement can issue you summonses for infractions and impound your boat just as if you were driving a car. The crazy thing is all you need to operate a boat is a boat registration. Other than that, you're on your way. It's crazy right? No safety class, no nothing.

Unfortunately every year we read about some poor person who loses their life on the water. It's understandable that the water can be an unpredictable and dangerous place, but some tragedies are avoidable.

If you're going sailing or boating, for God's sake can you please tell someone? Give your loved ones the heads up where you're going and your approximate return time. If they love you, they might actually realize you're missing and call the authorities.

Unless you're Scott Peterson, there really isn't a reason for not letting anyone know you're out on the water. Playing secret squirrel can delay a search and rescue that could save your life. Make sure the boat is in proper working order. I get pissed when I get a flat tire, so I'm sure there probably isn't a worse feeling in the world than being stranded out at sea.

Having the proper equipment on board is also key to surviving on the water. If you don't know what kind of equipment is required on a boat, ask someone. There are plenty of old men at your marina that are more than willing to chew your ear off and give you advice that just may save your life.

Bull Riding

Let's face it, anything having to do with bulls is dangerous. Bull riding, bull fights, and bullshitting the wrong guy can all be dangerous to your health. I equate watching bull riding to slowing down to view a bad car accident on the side of the road. You didn't plan on watching either but morbid curiosity takes over and you have no choice but to watch.

There's nothing like watching a man in a starched shirt and cowboy hat tied atop something as large and powerful as a locomotive, and knowing that this locomotive is pissed off.

Watching the beautiful ballet of man and bull is breathtaking. Tied atop a beast and flailing for your life like a helpless ragdoll, until you are thrown on your head. There isn't enough starch in the world to soften your landing. Bull riding has to be a chiropractor's dream.

The bulls in Pamplona have a much better time than the bulls here in the United States. The bulls in Pamplona get to run around for a few days with other bulls and unlimited targets to gore. It's the equivalent of going to Disney World for the weekend. Rodeo bulls are housed in large arenas and are forced to listen to country music and uninteresting conversation.

Confined to a metal chute, they wait for a tick to be strapped on their back as the anger mounts. Taunted by corn dog pointing flea market patrons, they wait for their opportunity for revenge. To add insult to injury, there are fucking clowns that get in the way of the bulls having a good time.

Once the guy in the cowboy hat hits the ground horizontally, a clown jumps out of a fucking barrel and insists on getting in the way of the bull finishing off his prey. It doesn't seem fair to the bull after all the shit they go through.

If you really want to ride a bull, go to a redneck bar and ride a mechanical one. You won't get gored but you will throw out your back and get hit in the head with a bottle. To me bull riding seems like the fast track to getting hooked on oxycodone for a broken coccyx.

Mountain Climbing

Mountain climbing is for those with a sense of adventure and a profound love of the great outdoors. They thrive on the ability to climb atop the summit of a mountain and view what appears to be an unlimited universe. The feeling of euphoria and accomplishment that you succeeded in something most would never have the balls to try must be exhilarating. And don't forget the smell of all the free unlimited mountain air!

If you're this far along in the book, you're either thinking that last passage was a misprint or that I had a stroke. Of course I don't believe that shit, I just wanted to see if you were paying attention. So let's get back to reality here and as the great Jackie Gleason once said, "And away we go…"

Mountain climbing is for those with a disposable income or for the young and incredibly naive. You either have too much time or money on your hands, or you're trying something dangerous to fulfill your life.

Most upper class men battling a midlife crisis will go out and buy a convertible sports car, only to be snickered at by those he drives past. Suburban housewives will obtain a realtor's license, never to sell a house, but only to tell anyone who will listen that they are a licensed realtor.

Either way there are a lot safer solutions in battling a midlife crisis. There are easier and more affordable ways to die than to fly to a faraway land after maxing out your credit card at the Bass Pro Shop for gear that will enable you to croak early.

I don't like the cold or insects so I don't see the point of mountain climbing no matter where or what time of year it is. Mountain climbing puts you at the mercy of a lot of things that are out of your control. Weather is always unpredictable and you could die just as easily from a mudslide caused by heavy rains, or you could be snowed in by an unexpected storm and are never heard from again.

If you're a novice or do not know the terrain, you're going to need a guide to take you up and down the mountain. How well do you really know this guy that you're relying on to take you up and down this mountain? How much do professional mountain guides make? I'm not knocking the profession but I'm also not trusting some Grizzly Adams looking guy with my life atop a mountain.

How about bears? They look cute on YouTube swimming in pools in Vermont but they are dangerous. When you're on a mountain, you're in their backyard and they will gnaw on your head or tear your arm out of its socket for laughs.

You purchased a can of bear repellant on eBay from a guy who makes it in his basement in the redneck part of New Jersey. Good luck with that, you're going to need it. Do you really think you will be able to keep your cool, locate your repellant, and successfully spray a charging bear in the face? An unexpected charging bear is the equivalent to an unexpected gunfight.

I have a lot of friends who were in gunfights with criminals during my twenty years of service in law enforcement. From what I have gathered from their experiences, when gunfire is exchanged and the lead starts flying, it's a crap shoot.

Cops are taught to shoot into the chest cavity or the center mass area of a person. Most gunfights happen at close range with only a few feet between adversaries. Gunfights are almost always a complete surprise to both parties and muscle memory plays a large role as to who is going to come out on top. Cops like to use the expression "Spray and Pray" because when the shit hits the fan, you do not really have a lot of time to focus and aim.

You're basically punching out your weapon and firing, hoping to hit something. It is usually the one that sees it coming first and can keep his cool with a little luck that will ultimately survive.

So you and your mountain climbing buddies are half way up Pikes Peak when nature calls and you have to take a leak. You find a spot and with your dick in your hands, pissing into the wind, you begin to admire the majestic view without a care in the world.

It's right around then that you hear branches snapping and the roar of a bear closing in on you like a heat seeking missile. You look over to the other idiot climbers and well recommended guide for help when you realize they are all running away in different directions.

Besides the charging bear, all you can see are the lovely bright colored North Face jackets disappearing into the woods in the background. It's just your luck that the bear has chosen you out of your party and is closing in quickly. Maybe it's the Paco Rabanne you're wearing?

Whether you realize it or not, your survival is totally up to you in this scenario. Do you think you can keep your cool, shake your dick and aim a can of spray at the charging bear, hoping you hit him between the eyes? Spraying a stream into a tree for practice is a lot different than when your adrenaline is pumping in a life and death situation.

Let's say you beat the odds and hit that fucker right between the eyes. You better hope that bear spray you purchased from the bozo in New Jersey isn't wasp spray. You may have just infuriated the bear even more.

At about the time you're being mauled, your friends are halfway down the mountain and already on their smart phones taking selfies and posting their near death experience on Facebook, not realizing or caring about what is happening to you. Hopefully that wonderful bearded outdoorsy guide you hired has GPS so they can find and airlift what's left of you to a local morgue or hospital.

Maybe you will beat the odds and survive a bear mauling. I'm sure looking like Rocky Dennis for the rest of your life is better than death, right? Here is an interesting question. Does bear repellent have an expiration date? Maybe that's something you should have looked into before you got yourself into this situation.

I have a couple of friends who are well off and decided to climb some mountain in Nepal. These two guys are no strangers to danger and thought traveling halfway around the world to jeopardize their lives would be a fun way to spend a couple of weeks. One guy owns his own plane and flies regularly, the other is a Vietnam veteran and is basically fearless.

Both of their spouses and business partners tried to talk them out of this new adventure to no avail. One guy's business partner had legal documents drawn up in the event of his sudden death, to determine how the business would be divided up. The other guy's family took out a large life insurance policy on him just in case.

They both received a series of vaccines against diseases that thrive in that part of the world. For those who don't know, there are no direct nonstop flights to Nepal. It took them several days of travel through the shittiest parts of the world to get there. Both men are in their fifties and froze their asses off. One became very ill from Nepalese cuisine, who would have thought?

Ultimately they made it back alive to tell their adventurous tales. I'm no doctor but I'm guessing in the grand scheme of things these two thrill seekers took a few years off their lives after having completed this fruitless activity of climbing a mountain.

Mountain climbing is for those who want the chance to freeze to death and be interred in freshly packed snow on the side of some cliff. They want the chance to laugh in the face of a bear or Yeti as it tears them limb from limb. Exhaustion, lack of proper gear, or running out of your supplies are some of the ways you can die during your climb.

I never liked the cold or snow, so I moved to Florida to get away from all that shit. Traveling out of your time zone at great expense and taking a lot of gear with you to climb some mountain is not a fun hobby to me. Too many things can wrong and you could catch a cold!

Scuba Diving

Scuba diving requires you to travel out to sea while lugging a ton of shit with you. From the air tanks to the anti-shark cage, everything associated with this sport is heavy. Schlepping all that crap onto a boat just to see some fish seems like a big pain in the ass. People travel miles out into the ocean, putting their lives in danger when they can just as easily go to an aquarium. They will tell you that coral reefs are beautiful or manmade reefs created from sunken subway cars provide sea life with a majestic home. If you like coral so much go to an overpriced beach shop and buy some. If you want to see a subway car, go to NYC.

Hopefully your air tank regulator works properly and like in parachute jumping, you better hope whoever maintains your equipment knows what they are doing. So much can go wrong when you scuba dive. Your tank can run out of air, or if you come up too fast you can get the bends and wind up relaxing in an iron lung for a while. How about those sharks you wanted to see? You didn't think the whole family would come, did you? The idea of suffocating or being attacked by sharks is not appealing to me. I am afraid of the dark and love air too much to scuba dive. If you want to see or touch exotic fish, go to Seaworld or your local fish market.

Heli Skiing

This sport should be called "Who wants to start an avalanche". Jumping out of a helicopter for any reason is dangerous. And who the hell wants to get into a helicopter anyway? Jumping out of a helicopter hovering 3,000 feet above virgin snow (or pow-pow as they call it) is absolutely crazy.

Heli skiing is another example of spending a lot of money to shorten your life. If you want the ultimate high, you might as well shoot heroin. The high is probably better and you have a better chance of surviving.

Whitewater Rafting

Whitewater rafting is nature's rollercoaster, speeding across an untamed river. Here we have five to ten people crammed into an inflatable raft wearing life preservers, ridiculous orange helmets, and clutching paddles. Squeezing people into an overcrowded raft on a river that moves at the speed of a flushing football stadium toilet sounds like a punishment to me.

What better way to die that from a serious head injury while riding the fast moving rapids? It's another example of people who need an adrenaline rush and who love to tempt Mother Nature. Unless you're Butch and Sundance running away from Joe LeFors, there's no reason to jump into a roaring river.

Why in the world would you want to sit that close to so many people just to scare the shit out of yourself? One of the reasons I don't like to fly is the close proximity to other people. Now you're surrounded by a pack of screaming idiots, bouncing up and down a river. The way those rafts jump around, it looks like a person can get launched out of there like a piece of bread in a toaster.

You wanted to look the part and hit the Timberland outlet store before your river run trip. Your cute yellow shirt, which you paid too much for, isn't going to do much for the Liberty Bell sized crack you're going to get in your head when it hits a jagged rock. Nor will it help you when your foot gets caught in the rocks as you fight to keep your head above the pure mountain water that's slowly drowning you because you fell overboard. But look on the bright side, the raft filled with your drunken friends will merrily continue its breathtaking journey downstream without you.

Maybe I'm wrong but aren't most fast moving rivers out in the middle of nowhere? That means travel and camping are involved so count me out. Any vacation that involves me taking gear to the middle of nowhere is not for me.

I have nothing against those who have a zest for life. People who have set routines and never try something new or exciting will live longer but are usually boring. Ever hang out with an actuary? Brilliant group of people, but having someone tell you the odds of how you are shortening your life every time you get a drink at a cocktail party can get old pretty quickly. On the other hand, hanging out with a guy who blows flames out of his mouth after every shot of Jager would get on my nerves too.

Fireworks

I am the biggest dickhead in the world to now be writing about the dangers of fireworks. If my parents were alive today, I'm sure I would still get an earful about my exploits with fireworks.

Fireworks are wonderful in the hands of trained professionals. Who doesn't like a professional firework show put to music? Invented by the Chinese, they have become such a part of our culture every Fourth of July. Every year people are killed or maimed because of fireworks. They're dangerous just on their own, but when you factor in other elements, they become a recipe for disaster.

What better way to end a summer evening barbecue than with some fireworks and a trip to the hospital? After a couple of drinks on the Fourth of July, someone will inevitably break out the fireworks and everybody is grabbing for them with both hands. Alcohol, darkness and trying to light a fuse, can you say missing fingers?

I hate to state the obvious but fireworks are made in China. Some of you are going to say that I'm being stereotypical, but it's true. Let's face it, our Chinese friends have been known to take shortcuts with their export products.

The arsenic flavored rawhide bones that have been slowly poisoning your dog. Those are from China. What about all that nice Chinese drywall they sent us that's now molding up and ruining our homes?

But for whatever reason, every summer we trust their quality control with fireworks, something that is designed to explode. They don't give a shit about their own people so do you think they care about us over here buying their shitty products? Try suing a Chinese company. Get back to me on how you did. My best bet is that they tell you to kick rocks, if they ever get back to you at all.

As a child I loved fireworks to the point where I thought of the Fourth of July as a second Christmas. My parents forbade my brother and me to play with fireworks, but like most kids we got our hands on them anyway.

The family who lived across the street from us must have purchased over a thousand dollars' worth of fireworks every Fourth of July. They would put on a drunken Grucci like performance, with someone inevitably getting shot in the back with an eight ounce rocket. As the sun began to set over every Fourth, my family and I would sit out on our front porch waiting for the spectacle to begin.

They would stumble out of their house and into the street, carrying large black plastic garbage bags filled with fireworks. About six to eight drunken men would fight for space in front of the house. They would all start yelling at each other that the other didn't know what he was doing.

It would start out amicably enough, with each man respecting the others' space. The group would hold their fire to admire another's rocket or mortar launched into the sky, trying not to step on the other shooters' toes. They played nice for a while practicing an unorthodox lane courtesy like a ritual you might see at your local bowling alley.

But as the homemade wine continued to flow, the group was transformed into a pack of armed and dangerous drunken mountain guineas. Loud broken English was heard everywhere. "Getta fuck outta the way, you sonova beech", "No you getta fuck outta the way" was yelled as the anarchy began to erupt into the street.

Old wounds were reopened and yearlong truces between family members were no longer honored. The smell of gunpowder and burnt flesh permeated the air and vendettas were carried out with extreme prejudice.

Rockets were no longer headed into the sky but were instead aimed horizontally at each other. Each man seemed to have his own cheering section of relatives from across the street. Old women dressed in long black dresses with large dangling crucifixes sat on concrete steps cheering on their favorite relative like it was a sporting event.

Grown men ran for their lives seeking refuge behind parked cars as rockets whizzed past their heads like gunfire. Cherry bombs and M80s were tossed underneath cars in an attempt to flush out hiding infidels who had surrendered back into the street.

One year a guy who worked for them earned the nickname "Joe Balls" when he was shot in the groin with a roman candle, illuminating him in brilliant colors. This was not Vietnam, it was The Bronx and ceasefires did not exist. These men fought until the last penny rocket was fired.

The best way I can describe this circus is to compare it to Walt Disney World's Pirates of the Caribbean ride. When you come down the flume, your barge passes through a battle of drunken pirates on ships yelling incoherently and firing cannons at each other.

When the smoke cleared, it looked like a burn unit across the street. Wives bandaged their husbands and sons with gauze and surgical tape. All they needed was a flag, a drum and a fife, because it looked like The Spirit of 1776 portrait. This went on every year when I was a kid and how no one got killed or seriously injured is beyond me. Maybe it was divine intervention or just dumb luck. But it was definitely entertaining.

The next day, the street always looked like a ticker tape parade had gone by. Littered with burnt paper and firework remnants, my brother and I combed the street for our gold nuggets. You see, what was left behind in this mess was very valuable to us. Unexploded fireworks (or duds) were left behind to be collected by my parents' two miscreants. With our parents off at work and my elderly grandparents unable to keep up with us, my brother and I came up with the idea to put on our own Fifth of July fireworks show.

We loaded up an old metal garbage can with unexploded ordinance and brought it into our tiny postage stamp backyard. Then one of us came up with the idea that those poor unexploded duds needed some help to get going. I poured out what was left of a gallon of milk into the sink and promptly walked over to the gas station. To this day it amazes me that they sold a ten year old kid fifty cents worth of gas in a plastic milk jug. As I walked home, I remember saying to myself how much the gasoline looked like fruit punch in that clear plastic container.

I poured the awful looking fruit punch into the garbage can, soaking the unexploded fireworks below. I then went into the house, walked past my grandparents who were watching *All My Children*, and grabbed a pack of my father's matches off the counter.

Back outside, my brother and I stood on either side of the garbage can like morons, unable to grasp how much danger we were in. When I lit the match there was a bright flash and a deafening roaring sound. I felt like someone had thrown an incredibly hot blanket upon me. When I opened my eyes and my hearing had returned, I was about 5 feet away from the garbage can which now resembled an exploding volcano.

My brother and I ran for our lives as rockets and whistlers were coming out of the garbage can in every direction. It seemed as if every couple of seconds the garbage can would burp out an unpredictable flaming explosive. When we reached the back porch, we were greeted by our immigrant grandparents screaming at us in a concerto of Italian and Yugoslavian.

As my grandmother beat us with a wooden spoon, my grandfather grabbed a hose to put out the inferno we had created. My grandfather already in his seventies and with a heart condition, felt bad for us and tried to clean up the crime scene. Grandpa was no Winston Wolfe however, so he left the blackened garbage can on the side of the house and burnt paper all over the yard.

Children have the memory span of pets and do not perceive the consequences of their actions. After our ass kicking at the hands of our grandmother, we figured everything was copacetic. Grandma resumed watching *All My Children* and grandpa served us soup on that hot July day.

After a hard day locked in a freezer and cutting meat all day, my poor father was in no mood to see that his tiny backyard had gotten trashed. The garbage can left what resembled a burn crop circle or a UFO landing site in the center of our lawn. Burnt bits of paper littered the yard like snowflakes.

We were summoned to The Hague for questioning while my grandparents pled for our lives. When I came downstairs from my spider hole to the commotion I saw a look of shock in my father's eyes.

"What happened to you, what's wrong with your eyes?" he asked my brother and me. My dad was looking at his two idiots with singed hair and no eyebrows. He examined us carefully with a pained look in his face. He probably wondered if he was going to have a lifetime of these scenarios and sent his two chemo kids to bed. You would have thought that almost getting blown up by a homemade IED would have taught us a lesson to stay away from fireworks. It didn't and as a matter of fact, it got worse.

We got older and were able to jump on a train to Chinatown to buy fireworks. Soon after, we got tired of traveling all the way downtown so we found a local connection. A mailman who lived about three blocks from us was selling fireworks out of his garage. Kids would line up in front of his house in the afternoon and wait for him to come home. The guy would get out of his car in his letter carrier uniform only to be swarmed by groups of teens lying in wait for him. This guy's garage was packed with every firework you could image. Looking back, I'm sure it was a fire hazard to store illegal fireworks in a hot garage. We would buy boxes or garbage bags full of fireworks and jump on our bikes with our booty and ride off to the beach.

Believe it or not there are beaches in The Bronx. Shitty ones with black sand and oily water and lots of rocks, but there are beaches. A friend of mine lived across the street from the beach and we would go over to the water with shovels and pieces of wood after the sun went down.

We would dig trenches and put wood ramparts above them to launch rockets and protect us from incoming fire. We also would bring long pipes and whiffle ball bats with the tops cut off to aim and launch our rockets. Two to four guys would occupy each trench about 60 to 70 feet from one another. Never once did it occur to us to wear eye protection, and now looking back we were begging to lose an eye.

Whistling bottle rockets with report were the best for scaring the shit out of your adversary, in my case, my brother in the other trench. Tired of losing, Fredo upped the ante and brought a pack of M80s to the battle one night. Lying in our foxhole with packs of open bottle rockets, we were engaged in an epic firefight with the enemy.

I remember as if it were yesterday when I saw my brother jump out of his trench and charge our foxhole, making himself a vulnerable target to our rockets. He yelled "For the cause!" and threw something lit at our bunker. You have to remember that it was pretty dark when this glowing object landed near our trench.

"Holy shit, your brother is fucking crazy!" my friend yelled, as the M80 went off about 15 feet away from us. I felt like I was in a silent movie for the rest of the battle. Fredo could have blown our hands off or worse if his aim had been better with that M80. My brother loved M80s and always seemed to find new and interesting things to do with them. He put them in garbage cans, sewers, and people's hallways.

Sometimes I wonder if the Unabomber got his ideas from my brother. Fredo would never want to trouble anyone to read his manifesto, he would much rather blow up your mailbox. I remember one time he walked up to a drive through speaker box and waited until they asked for his order. He then let his calling card explode next to the speaker, scaring the shit out of a handful of McDonald's employees.

Another way for us to pass the evening was Roman candle gunfights. My brother and I would square off about 20 feet from each other with Roman candles in both hands. Two of our enabler friends would act like our pit crews and would light each idiot's Roman candle fuses.

The rules were basically standing there rotating each Roman candle in a circular motion, hoping to get your flare out first and hit your mark before he got you. My brother was fearless and would stand his ground while I would retreat or try to get a better angle as the flares shot past my face.

One time he hit the back of my head with a flare and burned my hair. I had that burnt hair smell from July until October. Another time I hit him center mass in the chest, burning a large hole in his T-shirt.

Fireworks are a lot of fun but they are not worth the risk of losing your life or fingers. I know I am hypocrite, but leave those things alone because they are nothing but trouble.

At the risk of sounding like an old fart, I think today's young people get balls and stupidity confused a lot more than my generation did. When I was a child, we got the bumps and bruises early in life and learned valuable lessons about pain and common sense. We'd spend all day playing tackle football in the snow, climbing trees, or horsing around. We were knocked around but we learned from it.

In today's society children are raised in a bubble. Today's kids play video games and have no interest in going outside or using their imagination. Car seats, bike helmets, and shin guards lure children into a false sense of security that they won't get hurt. Growing up packed in Styrofoam peanuts, today's kids never really feel pain and are under the illusion that they are invincible.

I understand parents wanting to protect their children from injury. The problem though begins when a child is no longer a child and is away from the over-watchful eye of a parent. That's when all hell can break loose and the injuries are severe and sometimes fatal. Jumping off of something in a video game is a lot different than jumping off a bridge. Today's parents overly protect their children from the outside world, never giving any thought to who is going to protect their child from himself when they get older.

Playing video games and the insatiable urge to become famous on YouTube is a recipe for disaster. Sure, kids are going to get bumped and bruised but you're better off letting it happen now than getting a call from a hospital in the middle of nowhere when they're older.

There's a big difference between having the balls to do something dangerous and stupidity. Enlisting in the military or going into law enforcement and other dangerous occupations, you know there's a risk you can be killed. Be it for love of country or putting food on the table, there's a valid and logical reason behind it. To put your life in harm's way for nothing more than an adrenaline rush is crazy.

My father's words of wisdom to my brother from over thirty years ago ring true to this day… "Never confuse balls with stupidity".

Chapter 12

Social Irresponsibility

If you google the phrase "social irresponsibility", you will get pages of results accusing corporations and companies of committing a wide range of atrocities against the downtrodden, third world countries, and even mother earth. Wikipedia's definition of social irresponsibility also lectures us that it is everyone's duty to maintain a balance between the economy and ecosystems.

What a bunch of bullshit! My duty? Other than death and paying taxes, and there are plenty of free holes who don't do the latter, I have no duty other than to keep my own house in order. I'm sorry, I guess I must have missed that memo. I raised my hand and took an oath to uphold the constitution and to protect the citizens of New York City almost 30 years ago, nothing more nothing less.

"Economy and ecosystems" sounds like something a communist, corduroy wearing, silver haired ponytail professor would say while lecturing (or brainwashing) a bunch of college students. Reliving an acid trip from the sixties, he has the balls to lecture your kids about duty. This is the same guy who burned his draft card and ran off to Canada to get high, what a hypocrite. If you give him a chance, he will quote junk science to try and lead you to believe humans are an invasive species to the earth.

So when your financially dependent college student comes home on break, and calls you "socially irresponsible" for not sorting the recyclables while you're putting his ass through college, you now know where they heard it from. You will never guess who authored the overpriced textbook that you paid for, which is now the catalyst for your kid's animosity towards you… that's right, the socially responsible commie professor.

If you try to do the right thing in life, things will for the most part fall into place for you, especially living in this country. Remember what they taught us in school before all the politically correct bullshit; life, liberty and the pursuit of happiness. Pay your taxes, don't engage in behavior that attracts the police, and stay out of other people's business, and you will go far my son.

On the other side of the coin, I'm not saying for a second that corporations don't push the envelope to take short cuts when it comes to making money. Let's face it, they exist to make money. So do the mafia and drug cartels but they leave people dead in the street. But you won't see Wikipedia or bloggers saying how socially irresponsible they are. Nor will you see ambulance chasing attorneys having the balls to sue the mafia or drug cartels. I can't think of anything more socially irresponsible than murder, and if they leave a body in the street, that's littering too. I'm guessing a dead body left in the street leaves a larger carbon footprint than the aluminum can you didn't recycle.

I'm no Erin Brockovich, but I know that corporations are made up of people and some are quite greedy and immoral. Unfortunately some corporations get carried away when trying to grow their bottom line. The mind set becomes "If we can raise the bottom line by taking a shortcut and get away with it, let's try it".

During my twenty year career in law enforcement, I dealt with those who thought they could get away with something illegal or immoral and took the chance. Corporations are in the business to make money and we should be fine with that. But when they knowingly push the envelope with our safety and health, that is where we should draw the line.

Now of course corporations have a huge edge when taking shortcuts that backfire. First they will try plausible deniability, and if that doesn't work they let out the shark attorneys that they always keep on retainer. The little guy or consumer is up against a nameless, faceless entity who's armed with a tribe of attorneys. It's like the scorpion crossing the pond on the frog scenario, it's just their nature to see what they can get away with.

That's not to say there are those in society who will call an 800 number law firm looking to file a bullshit claim against a corporation. You can blame corporations all you want but they could never get away with half the shit they pull if it wasn't for the scumbags we send to Washington to represent us, who ultimately don't represent us at all.

Once those clowns are elected into office, they are bought and paid for. I'll bet you politicians never have to reach for their wallets again after they are elected. They are wined and dined at the finest restaurants by lobbyists who come out of the woodwork like roaches in a kitchen after the lights go out. The sad thing is they do it in broad daylight and it's perfectly legal. If a large corporation needs a new piece of legislature passed to help their business, you better believe they will pull a few boners in Washington to get the job done.

Corporations have our representatives' private numbers on speed dial. A few times I made it a point to call my congressman in Washington about something I felt strongly about. I got a young aid on the phone who asked me for my address and couldn't get me off the phone fast enough. Think twice the next time you're in a voting booth electing one of these bozos into office. If you want to believe corporations are evil so be it, but I think the people we vote for to represent us in both parties are a lot worse.

Back to Wikipedia's claim that it's my duty to maintain a balance between the economy and ecosystems. I'm not buying into that. The only duty I have is to be a decent person and stay out of trouble. Here is my definition of socially irresponsible.

Social Irresponsibility: A person who selfishly engages in a dangerous and unnecessary act, putting their life and the lives of others at risk for self-gratification. A socially irresponsible person has no regard for public safety, property damage, or the monumental cost that may be incurred as a result of their actions. A socially irresponsible person will often attempt dangerous and wonton activities, throwing common sense to the wind and endangering the lives of the first responders who attempt to rescue these jerkoffs from the predicaments they have gotten themselves into.

Close to Home

I was a typical child who loved sports, you name it, I played it. I got bumps and bruises but I never was the kid who was always in the emergency room. The biggest inconvenience I caused my parents from an injury was taking out the rubbing alcohol and a Band-Aid from the medicine cabinet. My parents had it easy with me as far as injuries were concerned. Then my younger brother Fredo came along. He didn't really enjoy playing sports, his passion was scaring the shit out of my parents.

I've said it before and I'll say it again, if there were home video cameras in the 1970s my brother would have been a YouTube sensation. He would have made Steve O and Johnny Knoxville look like a couple of Mormon kids just riding their bikes through a bad neighborhood. Fredo was my introduction into the world of socially irresponsibility.

Fredo's mission in life was to hurt himself, and the bloodier the better. He and his trusty sidekick Pinhead (yes that was his nickname, you are judged by the company you keep) spent countless hours in the emergency room after having hurt themselves and others.

The stupidity my brother exhibited seemed to have no end. Once at a local church, he and Pinhead had a contest to see who could jump down the most stairs at one time. Fredo won the competition and celebrated at the local hospital. His trophy was a cast for his broken leg.

Jumping rooftops or sliding down steep embankments off the cross Bronx expressway on stolen plastic covers used to cap sand barriers, Fredo was a stuntman without a movie. It got to the point where my father was tired of driving him to the hospital and using his Blue Cross Blue Shield insurance card.

"I'm tired of this shit" he told Fredo. "The next time you hurt yourself, you're on your own, you either take yourself to the hospital or treat yourself" my father said.

His other standard warning to us was "If you do that, Jesus Christ won't be able to save you". This was his way of giving us advanced notice of a pending ass kicking if we did something really bad. I'll say this about my father; you always knew what the rules were, though we often pushed the envelope.

A few months after the church stairs incident, my parents got a call from our middle school. The gym teacher had noticed a few abnormalities on my brother and had my parents come in for a chat. The gym teacher explained that Fredo had some unusual scars on his arm and leg and that he seemed reluctant to talk about his injuries.

Fredo had taken my father at his word about treating his own injuries and used my mother's needle and thread to stitch a few of his open wounds. The gym teacher probably thought my parents were running a Hanoi Hilton and were beating my brother and me with sharp bamboo sticks. My parents were embarrassed and justifiably horrified. Fredo almost got a concussion for his troubles at the hands of my father on the drive home. Like I said, I call him Fredo for a reason.

My brother never really grew out of his daredevil persona and he carries the scars as well as a long list of physical ailments related to his socially irresponsible behavior. Age hasn't stopped him either, he still engages in this type of behavior to this day.

Man has been doing ridiculous things to shorten his life ever since he decided to walk upright. If we evolved from apes maybe we should ask them for advice because other than climbing trees, they don't seem to get into the dangerous predicaments we humans do.

Leave the Daredevil Stuff to the Professionals

Living in The Bronx in the 1970s, cable wasn't yet available and even if it was, we couldn't afford it. There were only 5 television stations and none of them covered sports. ESPN hadn't hit the airwaves yet and if you were lucky, ABC's *Wide World of Sports* might have something interesting on Saturday. Besides the agony of defeat skier skiing into a tree, or the fat soviet weightlifter in red tights begging to drop a testicle while deadlifting a million pounds, we didn't have much of a sports outlet. By far Evel Knievel was the man.

We hoped and prayed Evel had made it out of the hospital from his last escapade to hurry up and jump something else. Fountains, double decker tour buses, and fat chicks… you name it, he jumped it. So was Evel Knievel socially irresponsible? His jumps were incredibly dangerous and kept the public at large mystified for hours on a Saturday afternoon.

I say the answer is no for a lot of reasons. First of all, people paid to see Evel Knievel and his jumps were covered on national TV. Rescue crews, ambulances and doctors were standing by and paid for by Evel or the network.

The idiot in the middle of nowhere armed with a GoPro and without access to medical aid or the means to pay for it is the guy I have a problem with. There was only one Evel Knievel and I actually met him in a bar in Florida in the early 90s. He was a really nice guy too and a lot smaller than I thought him to be.

Being a professional daredevil like a Cirque du Soleil performer who trains for hours at a time with safety equipment and has medical personnel on standby is one thing. God forbid they get themselves hurt or killed, they took precautions and are paid professionals who knew the risks of what they were getting themselves into. Here is a cast of characters who don't.

Free Solo Rock Climbing

You have to have the balls of an elephant to free solo rock climb. Free solo rock climbers use no harness, rope, or common sense while climbing million year old rock formations hundreds of feet into the sky. A pair of gloves and maybe a water bottle and they are on their way up a 90 degree angle like Spiderman. Even the great Nick Wallenda takes a pole with him when he's that far up. Rock climbers travel to national parks to climb majestic carved terrain that resembles the backdrop of an old western movie. The problem with climbing rock formations is nobody and I mean nobody can gauge the terrain. Those beautiful rock facades were made by millions of years of Mother Nature shaping them through her cycles of rain, sun, and wind. Just like Mother Nature's weather cycles, the rock wall surfaces are unpredictable. Why would you trust a several million year old rock wall with your life?

Getting stoned by a rockslide (and not reefer) is not the way anyone living in the twenty first century should die. Neither is falling off a steep ledge in the middle of nowhere. A 20 foot fall onto jagged rocks is more than enough to kill you, or at least turn you into Stephen Hawking leaving you to blow through a tube.

What happens when you're halfway up devil's tower and you have to take a dump? Do you hold onto the mountain with one hand, pull your pants down with the other, and let gravity do the rest? I have a hard enough time handling a book and toilet paper when I'm on the throne.

What if you're hundreds of feet in the air hanging onto the side of a large rock and it dawns on you that what you're doing is crazy? You get second thoughts and lose your balls instantly. There isn't going to be time for anyone to save you.

Let's say you're successful in your climb, you take a couple of selfies, now what? All you were able to take up with you on your 800 foot ascent was a bottle of Dasani and a power bar that tastes like ass. You have to come down at some point don't you? I mean how many photos can you really take? You're going to be hot and fatigued so please don't tell me the climb down is easier. You want to take the chance of seeing what really happens in the falling dream sequence we all have? You're not going to wake up before you hit bottom in this scenario. You better hope you have a friend who has a helicopter and is willing to rescue your ass.

Wasn't it was only a few years ago that some guy was rock climbing by himself and got his hand stuck in some ledge? He was there for days until he had to cut his own hand off with a pocketknife to free himself. He probably got the idea from the joke about the guy gnawing off his own arm to free himself from an ugly woman who was lying on top of him.

God forbid you do get hurt out in no man's land. Who is coming to get you, Nurse Betty? You have GPS and that's wonderful. Living in Florida, my GPS sometimes shits the bed so good luck deep in the woods of Yosemite National Park. If you really have to climb something so bad, go to the mall and climb a fake rock wall for a half hour. Its air conditioned so you won't sweat your ass off and afterwards you can treat yourself to Cinnabon on the way out.

Parachuting, BASE Jumping, and Hot Air Balloons

The thought of jumping out of a mechanically sound airplane high above the clouds for no other reason than for thrills is idiotic to me. I will admit that to parachute out of a plane for any reason, you have to have brass balls, though not necessarily brains.

Other than our brave servicemen and women who go through jump school to learn the art of jumping out of a plane to defend our country, I just don't see the point of it. If I really want to scare the shit out of myself for fifteen minutes, I would go out on a blind date with a woman who refused to post a profile picture on match.com. That encounter would be a lot shorter than someone jumping out of a plane, I can assure you that.

I do believe that it's an art to successfully jump from a plane. You have to take into account wind, the speed of the plane, and the terrain where you will land.

When an amateur goes skydiving, there is a lot of blind trust involved. You have to trust a pilot who isn't quite good enough to fly for a commercial airline. You have to trust a propeller plane that looks like it's seen better days and nobody seems to know anything about its origin. You have to trust the stoner who packed your parachute while on the phone with his weed connection. Do you think he noticed the tear in the seam of your chute? You have to trust a guy who spoons you like a new lover from the time you jump until you land and all the while you're hoping he pulls the cord at the right time. You also have to trust your new Siamese twin doesn't land the two of you into the path of a combine harvester going full speed ahead in some wheat field.

If you want to relive your experience, for another hundred bucks your Siamese twin will video you shitting your pants and crying for your mama. Spring for the video so that you can show all your friends what a moron you are!

Then you have the so called experts who skydive all the time. After a while, like anything else, that gets boring so what do humans do when they get bored?

They raise the bar and create new and interesting ways to die in what is already a dangerous exercise in futility. Five, ten, fuck it, twenty morons jump out of a plane all at once. I know this about strings, ropes and extensions cords; they always seem to get tangled together. Now add the equation of twenty idiots pulling cords at about the same time.

If that's not dangerous enough for you, how about forming interesting shapes with your fellow skydivers as you fall to earth? The more complex the shapes are, the better they feel about themselves. How about a trapezoid or isosceles triangle? What better way to die than to get your parachute cords tangled while forming unique math symbols with a bunch of strangers who flunked trig!

What if you still want to jump and do not like airplanes? There's great news for you, BASE jumping is a thing and it's the new phenomenon sweeping the world. BASE jumping is exponentially more dangerous than jumping from a plane high above some corn field. When you jump from a plane, you are jumping from a distance of between 8,500 and 13,000 feet. But when you BASE jump off some building or structure, it's usually nowhere near as high up, meaning you have no room for error. You won't have time to deploy a second chute in case of emergency.

Another downside of BASE jumping is that it's illegal. No one is going to give some dickhead a permit to kill himself by jumping from a high-rise building or bridge. Not only are these dickheads endangering themselves, but they put the public at risk with their ridiculous stunts. One mishap and a BASE jumper can slam into a building like an insect hitting a windshield, or land on some poor schmuck walking on the sidewalk.

What's unusual about this group is that it's not just about the thrill of the jump, it's also about the attention. Even if they pull off a dangerous BASE jump undetected, they feel the need to publicize it on the internet. The invention of the GoPro enables a moron with no common sense to become a YouTube internet sensation overnight.

I am a huge fan of GoPro and I think it's an ingenious product. But like with anything else, when you put something powerful in the hands of a moron, bad things will happen. Now you have a society of self-gratifying thrill seekers seeking notoriety with no regards for public safety.

Balloon riding is a lost art that should remain lost. It's just another facet of outdated stupidity we seem to love to hang on to. Why is it that we love to romanticize and revisit the days of yesteryear, putting our lives in peril? Technology is supposed to make our lives safer and better. So why do we insist on going back in time for the stupid and dangerous activities of the past?

If you really want to go back in time, use an outhouse or watch a silent movie. When something is proven to be dangerous and stupid we should acknowledge it, move on, and do something else. To continue doing it for no other reason than self-gratification is idiotic. Anyone ever hear the definition of insanity?

Who ever thought of flying a picnic basket suspended by a balloon into the sky must have been crazy. I don't proclaim to have a PhD in engineering or know anything about free falling object motion, but what I do know is when a heavy wicker basket filled with hundreds of pounds of people drops 1,000 feet out of the sky unexpectedly, the chances of survival are zilch.

Baskets are made for picnics not for transporting idiots into the sky. On top of that, how about the open fire powering this idiotic thing, blasting away just above your head? Would you put a wicker basket near your gas stove when you were cooking? If I had a dish towel near the stove in my mother's kitchen, she would go ape shit.

Did anyone ever consider wind into this equation? I get the shit scared out of me when we get turbulence in a plane. Imagine up in the clouds when the wind starts blowing and you begin to swing back and forth violently like a European going commando.

Ever give it any thought that it might get a wee bit choppy flying around in a swinging testicle? How about those pesky high power tension lines that always seem to get in the way? You hit one of those things in your flying basket and you're going to light up, snap, crackle, and pop like a mosquito hitting a fly zapper.

What happens if the balloon pops? It goes down and it goes down hard. A square heavy basket filled with people 1,000 feet up in the sky is not aerodynamically friendly. The balloon captain or whatever he's called is not going to glide that thing gently into a wheat field.

The days of balloon riding should have gone to the wayside with men in top hats and Rutherford B Hayes beards. People of that generation were just happy to see anything go into the air. If you're that desperate to fly something, go buy a remote control helicopter at Toys R US. I can think of a lot safer options for my entertainment dollar than to go for a balloon ride at the county fair. Don't people in the Midwest have anything better to do than sail across the Great Plains in a basket?

Here is a scientific safety equation put into layman's terms that hopefully may save some lives:

Height x Open flame x Wind x Electrical lines + Basket = Death

Balloon riding is not only dangerous for basket riders but also for first responders who have to free the entangled fried carcasses from power lines. If I am getting into a gondola, it's going be in Venice with a singing Italian and a pole. Balloons are for kids' parties or to be inhaled for a good time, not for carrying a basket of morons floating around aimlessly and without an exit strategy. If you really love balloons and baskets so much, go get a job at your local FTD florist.

I have nothing against adrenaline junkies who have a zest for life. It's the selfish amateurs who put the public or first responders at risk with their antics. If you want to be a dickhead and risk your life, that's fine, just make sure you don't get anyone else hurt and also make sure you have the medical coverage to pay for your broken ass.

Chapter 13

Home Alone

Home sweet home, it's the one place in the world where we feel safe from the dangers of the outside world. But are you really safe in your own home? I'm not talking about being the victim of a home invasion, I'm talking about self-inflicted stupidity.

Every year thousands of Americans are killed or seriously injured attempting some kind of home improvement project. They simply get in over their heads, take a shortcut, or just don't have the slightest idea of what they are doing. Despite an umpire's ruling, you're not always safe at home.

It all boils down to greed. Greed for time or greed for money, we are always trying to save a buck or take a shortcut to save time. When you avoid paying someone to do a job that you yourself are unskilled to do, bad things can happen very quickly.

Another big factor in getting killed or seriously injured around the house is going it alone. If you're doing a project alone in your home and something goes terribly wrong, who are you going to call for help, Bob Villa? He's trimming his beard somewhere and you can forget the Yankee clipper.

If a tree falls in the forest and nobody's there to hear it, does it make a sound? Well if you're yelling for help in your basement with a broken pelvis and nobody's there to hear you, what good does it do you? You're screwed, plain and simple. A man's home is his castle but unfortunately it can also be his death trap. Sometimes your house is not always the safest place to be. Think about it, so many things can go wrong just doing menial tasks around the house. Factor in working with tools, standing on a roof, or playing with electricity, and you have just significantly increased your chances of getting killed or hurt.

When you're in a rush, bad things can happen quickly. Something as ridiculous as eating your lunch too quickly while you're home alone can be deadly. Pressed for time today, you rush your lunch and shove a foot long cold cut hero down your throat. The Italian combo from Nunzio's deli has the freshest, softest bread. With cured meats and cheeses suspended from eye hooks in the ceiling, Nunzio's is a cardiologist dream. Anyway, you shove the last piece of sandwich in your mouth while rushing to do something else. As the prosciutto melts in your mouth, you realize something's wrong.

The soft bread and mozzarella that bring joy to your mouth have just lodged in the back of your throat like in a clogged toilet. At first you think you can swallow it, but it only goes deeper in. It has now formed a seal in your throat like an air tight gasket.

By now you should realize you don't have much time before you turn blue and suffocate. Nobody's home and the phone is useless because you cannot speak. You better hope in those last remaining minutes that your neighbor is home and has forgiven you for your dog crapping in his yard. Hopefully he answers the door and knows the Heimlich maneuver. It's really a pity something so delicious could wind up killing you.

Your bathroom is a home away from home, especially if you have kids or live with someone. Lock the door and you're in your own little biosphere. But your bathroom can also be a tile deathtrap. Taking a shower or bath with nobody home is another way many people get killed or seriously injured every year. Not having a handrail affixed to the shower wall or those rubber sticky things that look like shit at the bottom of the bathtub increases your odds of getting hurt, especially if you're elderly and "have fallen and can't get up". After smashing your head on the bathtub, you're going to wish you sprung for the medical alert system.

If you're Cleopatra of the bathroom and insist on having a portable radio plugged into the wall or a curling iron lying around a full bathtub, you're definitely going to get the most permanent of perms.

Most are killed or seriously injured doing work around their homes. The reason being is we are scrambling around to complete multiple projects over the weekend. Rushing around, not paying attention, and fatigue are all contributing factors to getting injured or killed.

Just because you have a plumber's crack doesn't make you a plumber. How many times have you heard someone say "I'm not paying that guy" or "I can do that myself" when referring to some kind of home improvement project? The question is can you go without hiring a professional to complete a project and do it yourself without fucking it up or getting yourself killed? Or more importantly, should you?

Home Improvement Stores

Home improvement stores challenge our egos every day by running commercials that dare us to attempt dangerous projects that no sane person should attempt. They show average Joes like you and me tiling bathrooms, landscaping, or hanging ceiling fans. They make everything look so easy, don't they? You tried hanging a ceiling fan last year and it resulted in a hole in the ceiling and the death of the family dog, but that's not going to stop you from trying again.

What kind of man are you? You can save money by doing it yourself! "If that schmuck on TV can do it, why can't I" you say to yourself. You're a man, strong like a bull, you can do it. You head out of the house, full of piss and vinegar in route to your local home improvement store.

Visit any home improvement store over the weekend and you'll see a plethora of middle aged men wandering the aisles looking for someone to help them, like orphans in search of their birth mothers. They've successfully ditched their wives and have fled their homes like escaped convicts. Stepping into a home improvement store, they feel like they have entered a fortress of solitude.

Superman had Jor-El to advise him in his ice fortress. The problem is you have a better chance of finding a scarecrow, tin man, or cowardly lion than getting sound advice from an hourly paid employee at your friendly neighborhood home improvement store, I mean Oz.

Try to grab the attention of a flying monkey in an orange apron. You have a better chance seeing Halley's Comet twice in your lifetime. He definitely sees you trying to make eye contact to ask for help. Behaving like a guy who owes you money, he does an about face and pretends to respond to an inaudible announcement coming from the loudspeaker high above. He and his mullet turn the corner of the aisle with the grace of a gazelle gliding across the Serengeti. You're in full pursuit, well as fast as a middle aged guy with a gut can go. You turn the corner and just like Keyser Soze poof, he is gone.

Let's say you hit the lottery and actually corner one of the flying monkeys. You're either going to get "I don't know" or the quick dismissive "Yeah that should do it" standard answer to any question you may have. Neither response should leave you with confidence. The glazed look in his eyes is an indication the advice he is giving you in a possible life or death situation is bullshit. If your doctor gave you a diagnosis with the same indecisiveness or uninterested tone about a pain you were having in your chest, would you walk out of his office feeling relieved?

On the other side of the coin, you may get the overly helpful old man. He's decided to have a second career at your local home improvement store. Wearing a hearing aid and knowing nothing, he won't bullshit you. But what he will do is walk you all over the store like a Japanese tourist in Manhattan seeking the other flying monkeys trying to avoid you.

After a couple of hours of dealing with these jokers, your head is spinning as you walk out of the store pushing a shopping cart loaded with a machine that is going to maim or kill you. You get the contraption home and attempt to read the directions. This thing is like a Chinese menu, complete with spelling mistakes. The diagrams make no sense but you plug along with the assembly of the electric finger remover.

Your best bet trying to fix or figure something out around the house is YouTube. In addition to teenagers lighting farts or running around with dog shock collars on, YouTube is actually a wonderful source of information. Visit the YouTube website and look up whatever you've purchased or whatever project you're attempting around the house. There are numerous videos showing everything from installing a garbage disposal to assembling a pressure washer. Watch a few of the videos before you decide to use a circular saw to cut a metal pipe to avoid it resulting in your leg amputation.

The Lawn Ranger

You fired your landscaper because he had the audacity to raise your bill by five dollars a month. He's been loyally cutting your lawn for the last twenty years, four times a month for $75, never raising the price before now. You say to yourself "so what if the price of gasoline has gone up 50% since you hired him 20 years ago, what am I a schmuck?" He has some pair of balls trying to recoup his expenses. He's crossed the line and you've had enough. Screw him, you're going to cut your lawn yourself.

But when was the last time you used your lawnmower? Maybe 20 years ago? You take the blade off the mower and run it over to the hardware store where a flying monkey sharpens it for you. You improperly slap the blade back on without the washer and don't bother to tighten the lock nut sufficiently.

Pushing a mower around the lawn gives you a sense of pride. You're saving money and getting exercise at the same time you think to yourself. "Why did I pay that jerkoff landscaper all those years for?" Half the time the Mexican army did a half assed job cutting my lawn anyway.

Your shit eating grin begins to fade when your mower starts making a strange sound. Moving at three hundred revolutions per minute, the blade you improperly installed spins out of the shroud, severing off a few of your toes and ruining your new Birkenstock Jesus sandals in the process. You really should have worn something better on your feet. There goes your chance of getting on *Dancing with the Stars.*

Let's say you decide to take on the whole backyard by yourself. How dangerous can trimming your hedges be? You buy a used hedge trimmer at a yard sale instead of purchasing a new one. As you're slicing through your hedges, you think "this is so easy. "Once I get the hang of this, I'm going to carve my hedges into Disney characters".

Swinging the old relic hedge trimmer like a lightsaber, your sweaty and fatigued hand loses its grip. The trimmer begins to fall out of your right hand when muscle memory kicks in. Instinctively, you grab the falling blade with your left hand. The only problem is this old machine will not stop sawing after the trigger is released.

Watching your fingers fall to the ground must be a terrible feeling. You better hope your neighbor's ice maker is working and that he has sandwich bags to pack your fingers in for the ride to the hospital. Look on the bright side, with your missing or deformed fingers you can always get a job operating poorly built rides as a carney at the county fair.

What Goes Up Must Come Down

What goes up must come down applies to ladders, big time. Depending on how you go up has a lot to do with how you come down. Coming down incorrectly might just get you a broken neck. Even if you survive a broken neck, you're going to wear a halo contraption screwed into your head making you look like your head is in a birdcage. You can't even wipe your own ass when you're wearing that thing. But I hear you're supposed to get better TV reception because it doubles as an antenna.

You don't even have to fall off a ladder to get killed. Leaning a metal ladder against electrical lines or touching live wires with your head or hands is going to transform you into a Roman candle. Imagine the headache it's going to cause.

A lot of times people set up ladders with danger right beneath them, look no further than the cover of this book. Think of all those fun things below you, awaiting your landing. It's bad enough to fall 5 feet off a ladder but when you impale yourself on a wrought iron fence, you've entered the cul de sac of pain.

If your ladder is not tall enough to get you where you have to go, STOP and reevaluate what you're doing. You need to get a taller ladder, period. Don't improvise and put the ladder on a picnic table or stack bricks under each leg in an attempt to reach those few extra feet. Go to your home improvement store and just spend the few extra bucks on a new ladder. The risk of death or permanent paralysis is not worth the few bucks.

Madame Curie Syndrome

Playing mad scientist at home will also get you killed. If you failed chemistry class in high school, why would you attempt your comeback as a chemist now?

Whatever kind of floor cleaner you use on a tile floor never works. The grout is still going to look like shit no matter what the bottle promises. You think to yourself, "if one chemical doesn't work, how about trying two?" Rummaging around under the sink you find 2 of the strongest household chemicals known to man, ammonia and bleach. You didn't have time to read either bottle, which warn that mixing one chemical with the other is a big no-no, so you pour both liquids into your bucket.

Congratulations, you've just created deadly cyanide gas. This is a chemical compound used to execute condemned inmates on death row and not usually recommended to clean floors. Your bucket has become a witch's cauldron, "double bubble toil and trouble", and you watch the foggy cloud rising from the bucket and onto the floor. The warm vapor resembles a mushroom cloud and you say to yourself "why is this liquid hot?"

You did get a D in chemistry didn't you? You start to feel sleepy and all of a sudden you pass out, slamming head first into the foggy bottom of the floor, landing next to your dead cat. Worst of all, your tile floor will still look like shit.

Ben Franklin Didn't Know Any Better but You Should

It never ceases to amaze me how people with no knowledge or respect for something as dangerous as electricity play with it anyway. Electricity can kill you quickly or slowly. Just because you didn't get electrocuted wiring a new ballast in the garage, doesn't mean the electrical fire that will start in your ceiling three nights later won't kill you. But why worry, your house is equipped with smoke detectors. Oh wait, as you die from smoke inhalation, you remember that you removed the nine volt battery from the smoke detector five years ago because its beeping was keeping you up at night.

How about having the best of both worlds, playing with electricity *and* water? Installing hot water heaters, hot tubs, and dishwashers can also ruin your day if you don't know what you're doing.

You don't have to be color blind to get killed while playing around with electrical wires. Most people are killed when playing with electricity in their homes because they forget to do one simple thing. They neglect to locate the breaker box and shut power off to whatever device or outlet they're working on.

But why would you do that when you have a burned out test light? It's been sitting in the bottom of your tool box for the last fourteen years with all sorts of crap piled on top of it. Why go to a hardware store and trouble a flying monkey to find a new test light when this one will do.

Locate the circuit breaker box in your home open and inspect it. If you see round glass fuses instead of switches call a licensed electrician. This is not the time to use the logic "How smart could Thomas Edison be if he's dead?" and try to fix or service your outdated electrical fuse box yourself. I wouldn't put my hand anywhere near an old outdated fuse box. If there are pennies shoved into the slots where the glass fuses should be, run, don't walk, and call the fire department immediately.

Try selling a house with a Tesla invention doubling as a fuse box. See how well that goes during a house inspection. Speaking of getting electrocuted, here is an interesting fun fact. Every now and then homeless people living in subway tunnels are electrocuted when they piss on the third rail. Piss, like water, is a fine conductor of electricity and will blow your cock off if it touches electricity. So if you're homeless reading this book, don't be a dickhead by pissing on the third rail.

Your garage is an excellent place to die if you're not paying attention to what you're doing. How about starting your car in the closed garage while taking that important cell phone call? You should start feeling groggy from the carbon monoxide after about ten minutes and be brain dead by minute fifteen.

How about going up into the attic in July instead of calling the exterminator to investigate what's making all the noise up there? You know there's some kind of vermin up there having a party. Instead of calling the guy with the big plastic rat on the hood of his truck, you want to play crocodile hunter and venture into your hot dark attic alone. You're going to trap the wild beast that has violated the sanctity of your home all by yourself.

Armed with a flashlight and glue traps, you think you're ready for a bear or whatever else is up there. This time you even remembered to wear your old football helmet to save yourself from being scalped by the old nails jutting out of the roof's beams. Nothing is worse than a hot attic in the summer. Pitch black, filled with dust and pink insulation that doubles as itching powder, it's worse than a jail cell. Hopefully you enjoy your baked heart attack because the paramedics or funeral home personnel are going to have a hell of a time removing your body from the attic.

If you're going to embark in some kind of home improvement project for the first time, make sure you have someone around to either guide you or call an ambulance in the event you get in over your head. If you have the money, pay a professional to do something dangerous because taking a shortcut to save money may also shorten your life.

Chapter 14

The End

My late father used to call my brother and me "dick" or "dickhead" when we did something stupid starting in our teens all the way up until his death. Born in the 1940s, he had a wonderful sense of humor and once told me he was the originator of hurling the insult "dick".

I laughed and told him there was no way that could be proven, but he swore he did until the day he died. So If you're wondering where the title of the book came from, there you go.

I want to thank Gladys (who describes herself as pear shaped) for editing my book and dealing with my numerous, redundant emails. I also want to take a moment to thank all of you for purchasing my book. Hopefully some of you will have laughed and maybe learned something at the same time.

Some of you will think I am a judgmental prick and that's fine because it's your right to do so. I am without sin because as an accomplished dickhead, I have done many of the ridiculous things I'm now preaching you should avoid.

Here is an incomplete list of stupidity I have engaged in during fifty something years:

- Attempted to cross the Long Island Sound in an inner tube

- Trapped myself on a roof for 2 hours after my ladder fell over
- Dated mentally unstable women
- Patrolled the streets of NYC without wearing a bulletproof vest
- Piloted a boat with no experience, in the dead of night, after the lunatic captain became inebriated
- Frequented dive bars
- Tossed lit fireworks like they were bean bags
- Was chased by the cops when I was a teenager
- Detonated airbags under coworkers' desks
- Wrote a book about the ridiculous things I've done

Glossary

El sol: the sun

Paper asshole: a paper cutout used to line toilet seats to save your ass from crabs and other pathogens

Glass dick: crack pipe

Tune up: beat down or ass kicking, on unnecessary hospital visit

Cotton top: white haired geriatric

Mamaluke: Sicilian term for someone who engages in stupidity on a regular basis

Martinized: a dry cleaning method

Hairy eyeball: a dirty look or hard stare

Cock diesel: prison term used for a muscular inmate who runs the recreational yard

Chifferobe: an armoire-like piece of furniture usually found in the deep South, passed on from generation to generation

Speed loader: a circular device that holds six bullets, used to load a revolver

Roach coach: a mobile food truck used to spread salmonella

Jewish Navy: the United States Coast Guard

Mr. Hankey: A singing piece of fecal matter, derived from the cartoon series *South Park*

Pinched: to get arrested

Bullpen: large jail cells used to accommodate a multitude of prisoners awaiting arraignment in the NYC court system

The can: prison

Huevos grandes: big balls

Going commando: not wearing underwear, free balling

About the Author

Vic Ferrari is a retired 20 year veteran of the New York City police department. A Bronx resident for over 40 years, he now resides in sunny Florida eating subpar food and is forced to listen to country music. He enjoys writing, cooking, and his trusty sidekick, an Irish wolfhound who regularly ignores him.

Made in the USA
Middletown, DE
06 May 2024

53919336R00138